F

Gar

MW01125970

Book 21

Hope Callaghan

hopecallaghan.com
Copyright © 2018
All rights reserved.

*****

**Visit my website for new releases and special offers:
hopecallaghan.com**

Thank you, Peggy H., Cindi G., Jean P., Barbara W., Wanda D. and Renate P. for taking the time to preview *Framed in Florida,* for the extra sets of eyes and for catching all of my mistakes.

A special THANKS to my reader team!

Alice, Amary, Barbara, Becky, Brinda, Cassie, Charlene, Christina, Deb, Debbie, Dee, Denota, Devan, Diann, Grace, Helen, Jan, Jo-Ann, Joyce, Jean K., Jean M., Katherine, Lynne, Megan, Melda, Kat, Linda, Lynne, Pat, Patsy, Paula, Rebecca, Rita, Tamara, Valerie, Vicki and Virginia.

Allie, Anca, Angela, Ann, Anne, Bev, Bobbi, Bonny, Carol, Carmen, David, Debbie, Diana, Elaine, Elizabeth, Gareth, Ingrid, Jane, Jayne, Jean, Joan, Karen, Kate, Kathy, Lesley, Margaret, Marlene, Patricia, Pauline, Sharon, Sheila and Susan.

CONTENTS

Cast of Characters

Gloria Rutherford-Kennedy. Recently remarried, Gloria is the ringleader of her merry band of friends. She lives on a farm on the outskirts of Belhaven, a small town in West Michigan.

Lucy Carlson. Gloria's best friend. A bit of a weapon's expert and part-tomboy, Lucy enjoys shooting guns, riding four-wheelers and hunting...when she's not being dragged into one of Gloria's mysteries.

Dorothy Jenkins. Dorothy "Dot" Jenkins and her husband, Ray, are co-owners of Dot's Restaurant. The cautious one of the bunch, Dot would much rather stay on the sidelines during Gloria's adventures but most of the time it doesn't work out that way.

Margaret Hansen. Recently widowed, Margaret is learning to adjust to life alone. The most critical of the group of friends, Margaret tends to see everything in black and white with a tad of jaded.

Ruth Carpenter. Head postmaster of the Belhaven Post Office, Ruth is the queen of surveillance and is always up on the latest spy equipment. With her recently tricked out / customized, bulletproof van along with her high tech spy gear, Ruth is Gloria's right hand gal in many of her investigations.

Andrea Malone. The youngest member of the Garden Girls group, Andrea met Gloria and the others through a string of tragic events. Despite the fact that Gloria is protective of her young friend, Andrea is usually in the thick of all of Gloria's investigations.

"Charm is deceptive, and beauty is fleeting; but a woman who fears the Lord is to be praised."
Proverbs 31:30 (NIV)

Chapter 1

"Can I have your attention, *please?*" Ruth Carpenter scowled at her friends as they continued chattering amongst themselves.

"That does it." She wedged the whistle between her lips and blew two sharp toots.

The chattering stopped.

"Much better. Before we head to the airport to start our week-long, fun-filled vacation, I want to go over a few things."

"Oh brother," Lucy muttered under her breath.

"Here we go," Gloria whispered.

"The back of my van has limited space to stow our luggage and I want to make sure everyone is bringing one carry-on bag."

"I have one carry-on, but I got a big purse too. It's goin' with me or I'm not going," Rose said.

"Purses don't count." Ruth began counting the luggage, lined up next to her van. "Perfect. It looks as if there's only one piece per person." She nudged one of the larger pieces with the tip of her shoe. "This piece is bigger than the others."

"It's a standard carry-on piece. I've been using it for years." Margaret, fed up with drill sergeant Ruth, lifted her chin. "If you don't think there's enough room in your van, I can drive myself."

Ruth, noting the look on Margaret's face, softened her tone. "I didn't mean anything by it, Margaret. I'm sure it will fit just fine."

"Ruth wasn't picking on you. She's a little stressed out. We're all a little stressed out." Gloria attempted to smooth things over. Bickering before leaving home was not an ideal way to start their vacation.

The group of friends had been planning their trip to Florida for the past several months. Ruth volunteered to coordinate the vacation, and other than hints of a few days at a luxurious beachside resort, the women were clueless about what she had in store for them.

"No offense taken." Margaret smiled warmly. "Thanks for planning the trip, Ruth. I can't wait to find out where we're going."

"The sooner we hit the road, the sooner you'll find out." Ruth opened the van's rear doors and began loading the luggage. Arranging the pieces were akin to fitting puzzle pieces together and Ruth was right...space was limited. The entire rear of the van was floor-to-ceiling luggage.

She shoved the last piece on top and slammed the doors shut. "We better get a move on."

During the ride to the airport, the women discussed the upcoming trip and several of the friends threw out guesses on where they were going.

Gloria didn't care. She was thrilled at the prospect of spending time with Dot, Margaret, Lucy, Ruth and Rose. Eleanor, an elderly Belhaven resident, was also tagging along and Gloria was almost as excited for Eleanor as she was for herself. The only person missing was Andrea, whose baby was due in a few short weeks.

Eleanor had never flown on an airplane before. She told them it had been years since her last trip to Florida with her husband, Matthew.

"Are you ready for our big adventure?" Gloria asked.

"Oh yes." Eleanor pulled a piece of paper from her purse and unfolded it. "I've been keeping track of the clues Ruth gave us, and I'm pretty sure I'll be able to tick a few things off my bucket list."

Dot chuckled. "I can't wait to hear them."

"I've already told Gloria and Ruth." Eleanor cleared her throat. "At the tippy top of my list is riding along the beach in a convertible with the top down and the wind blowing through my hair."

"I would love to see all of us crammed in a convertible cruising the beach," Lucy laughed.

"We won't fit," Margaret chimed in. "Unless we sit on each other's laps."

"I promised Eleanor I would do everything in my power to make that happen and I think I've got it covered," Ruth said confidently.

"This trip is growing more exciting by the moment," Dot groaned.

Eleanor continued. "Next on my list is either skydiving or parasailing. I figure I have a better chance of parasailing since we'll already be close to the water."

"Or on the water," Ruth mumbled.

Margaret, who was sitting in the front passenger seat, turned to Ruth. "What did you say?"

"Nothing. Just talking to myself. Like I said; you'll find out soon enough, which reminds me...after we pick up our rental van, we need to pick up a few supplies. Sorry, Eleanor. Carry on."

"Yes, well. I only have a couple more things. Riding in an airplane is on the list. I have my camera ready to snap some photos to put on my bucket list bulletin board. Seeing a real live gator up close is near the top, too." Eleanor folded her note. "I was also thinking it would be fun to solve a mystery, but that might be pushing it."

The women let out a collective groan.

"Oh no." Rose firmly shook her head. "We ain't gettin' ourselves involved in no kinda mystery. Not on this trip. This is all about rest and relaxation."

"I'm with you, Rose," Ruth said. "I say we save the mysteries for home. We're here."

Ruth circled the terminal until she found their gate. She waited until the others exited the van and unloaded the luggage.

"We'll wait right here," Dot promised.

"I'll ride to the parking garage with you." Gloria hopped in the passenger seat and pulled the door shut.

"You don't have to go with me." Ruth checked her side mirror before pulling back into the traffic flow.

"I don't mind. We'll be sitting on the plane for a few hours. It will be good to do a little walking. Thanks again for planning our trip. I know it was a lot of work."

A frown flitted across Ruth's face. "I hope I didn't mess up."

"Mess up?"

"What if everyone hates my surprise? We paid good money, not to mention taking time away from work and our families to go on this trip."

7

"I'm sure it will be wonderful. Besides, if we don't like what you planned, rest assured we'll never put you in charge of our vacations again," Gloria joked.

"Right?" Ruth circled the parking garage until she found the perfect parking spot. She backed the van into the spot, squeezing in between two concrete posts. "That should keep the spymobile safe from door dings."

It was a quick walk back to the unloading zone, and the women found their friends in the same spot they left them. They all stepped inside and joined the long boarding line. Thankfully, it moved quickly and after picking up their boarding passes, they made their way to the back of the security line.

Ruth, followed by Gloria, Dot, Lucy, Margaret and Eleanor, sailed through security. Rose was the last to go through while the others waited on the other side.

Gloria grabbed her shoes off the conveyor belt and carried them to a nearby bench to put them on.

"We have a problem." Lucy began frantically waving and hurried over. "It's Rose."

Chapter 2

Gloria shoved her foot into her shoe. "A problem?"

"Two TSA agents pulled Rose out of the line and escorted her to a security screening room."

"Uh-oh." Gloria sprang to her feet and joined the others, hovering on the other side of the scanner. "Where is she?"

"Inside that room." Dot pointed to a door. "We can't go back. We're already through."

Ruth consulted her watch. "I hope this doesn't take long. We're cutting it kinda close."

"Great," Margaret groaned. "What could have set off the TSA's machines?"

"Rose's potions," Gloria and Dot said in unison.

"I warned her not to try to carry them on," Dot said. "She wouldn't listen to me."

"Rose is a smooth talker." Lucy waved her hand. "Let's hope she's able to talk her way out of this one."

Gloria's armpits grew damp as she gazed at her watch and then back at the door. "This isn't good."

"Try texting her cell phone," Eleanor suggested.

"Good idea." Ruth pulled her cell phone from her pocket and switched it on. She tapped out a message and waited. Rose didn't reply.

Another ten minutes passed and finally, a solemn faced TSA agent, accompanied by a flushed Rose, exited the room and made their way to the body scanner. The agent motioned for Rose to go inside and then placed her large purse on the conveyor belt.

Gloria nearly passed out when a light above the scanner flashed red. Thankfully, the agent who was with Rose motioned the person scanning the bag to let it go.

Rose stepped out of the body scanner and snatched her purse and shoes off the conveyor belt. "Sorry, everyone."

Gloria waited until they cleared the security area. "What happened?"

"My potions set off the alarms. The agent took me to a room where he tested them for explosives and drugs." Rose shook her head. "I tried to tell him they're herbal concoctions. He wouldn't listen and went ahead and tested them anyways."

"How...how many did you have in your purse?" Eleanor asked.

"Six."

"Good grief," Dot groaned.

"I originally packed eight. Johnnie made me leave a couple of them behind because he said they looked suspicious." Rose slipped her shoes on. "I guess he was right."

Gloria was curious. "Suspicious in what way?"

"He said they looked like marijuana."

"That would've done it," Ruth snorted. "I can guarantee if the agents thought you were trying to sneak pot on the plane, you would get a vacation all right...right here in the Kent County jail."

"Well, you better hope you don't get a sunburn or heat rash," Rose huffed. "We're plum out of luck."

"We need to get a move on, folks," Ruth said. "I'm sure they're boarding the plane."

"There's no way I'm gonna miss this flight." Eleanor flew by them. "No offense, Rose, but I would've left you behind."

The women picked up the pace and hustled through the terminal until they reached their gate and joined the long line.

Gloria was the last of their group to begin the long trek down the jet bridge and finally, they were on board the plane.

"It looks like we're sitting together." Eleanor waved her boarding pass at Gloria. "Do you mind if I take the window seat?"

"Not at all." Gloria watched as Eleanor settled into her seat. She slid the shade up and peered out. A small section of the wing blocked her view, but not by much.

"Are you ready for this?"

"Oh yes." Eleanor's eyes lit. "I haven't felt this alive since...well, since the time we almost got busted sneaking around Judge Judd's place a while back."

Eleanor placed the palm of her hand on Gloria's cheek. "I'm so excited my hands are sweating."

The jet bridge pulled away and the plane rumbled down the runway. Gloria closed her eyes. Taking off was her least favorite part of flying. She felt the thump of the wheels going up and when she opened her eyes, Eleanor was grinning from ear-to-ear. "That was so cool. You missed it."

"That's okay. Takeoffs aren't my favorite."

The flight was smooth, except for a small amount of turbulence over Georgia. Gloria thought Eleanor might be scared, but the older woman was thrilled with the jostling and didn't mind a bit.

"I want to check out the bathroom." Eleanor unbuckled her seatbelt.

"I think it's in the back. They're cozy," Gloria warned.

"I read up on the restrooms and wanted to see for myself if they're as small and smelly as everyone claims they are. I want to take a picture." Eleanor patted her pocket.

"I don't think you'll be disappointed." Gloria unbuckled and stepped into the aisle. Eleanor crawled over the seat and headed to the back of the plane.

She returned a short time later and Gloria waited until they were both seated. "Well? Was it everything you hoped it would be?"

"And more." Eleanor's head bobbed up and down. "I almost couldn't go. The toilet seat was vibrating. I might have to check it out again during the flight home."

"Of course."

Eleanor began to hum as she stared out the window. "I think we're getting close. I see water."

A short time later, the plane began its descent and soon, they were on the ground.

The sprawling Orlando airport terminal was confusing. After exiting the tram, the women took several wrong turns before figuring out they needed to take the escalators to the lower level and a shuttle bus to the car rental agency.

Ruth handled the rental like a pro, quickly collecting a large and luxurious van. They loaded their luggage in the back and there was even a little extra space left over.

"Perfect. We still have room to pick up our extra supplies."

"Are we going to stop at a Meijer store?" Dot asked.

"There are no Meijer stores in Florida," Ruth said. "We're gonna have to go to Wal-Mart or one of the big box home improvement stores."

"What about food?" Gloria patted her stomach. She'd skipped breakfast that morning, and the small bag of peanuts the flight attendant handed out on the plane was long gone.

"I have a grocery list. I think we can pick up everything at Wal-Mart instead of making more than one stop. I'm hoping to find one close to our destination. We'll need ice and I don't want it to melt."

"Where are we going?" Margaret asked.

"To the St. Johns River."

"The St. Johns River?" Gloria's breath caught in her throat. "We aren't going to the ocean?"

"In a roundabout way," Ruth said evasively. "Enough with the questions. I need to focus on driving."

They sped along the highway until finally reaching their exit, which was east of the airport. Gloria spotted several signs for the beach. It gave her a glimmer of hope perhaps Ruth was messing with them and they were headed to a seaside resort.

Her hopes were dashed when they passed by a roadside sign, *Daytona Beach, 33 Miles*. Ruth exited the highway at the next off-ramp. "I guess we're not going to Daytona Beach?"

"Nope." Ruth shook her head. "Not even close."

After a couple of turns, Ruth steered the van into the store parking lot. "I have two lists...a food list and a supply list. I say we divide and conquer. Who wants to pick up the food?"

"I will." Dot reached for the list.

"Great. I'm going to pick up the supplies since I have a better idea of what we need." Ruth, along with Gloria, Lucy and Eleanor headed to one side of the store while Dot, Rose and Margaret headed toward the food aisles on the other side.

Gloria's level of concern increased with each item Ruth added to the cart. She tossed in a can of bug spray, citronella candles, a pack of cheap flashlights, two foam coolers and batteries. "What about sunscreen?"

"Oh yes. We definitely need sunscreen." Ruth steered the cart to the seasonal aisle and added the sunscreen, along with a pair of cheap flip-flops. "You might want to save your good sandals for the second part of our trip. Flip-flops will work best for the next few days."

Gloria grimaced, but did as Ruth suggested and tossed in several one-size-fits-all for her and the others.

19

"I say we buy an extra pair, in case someone blows out their flip-flop." Eleanor added an extra pair to the pile. "This is so much fun. I can't wait to find out what we're doing. Can we build a campfire? It looks like we might be going camping."

"We're not going camping, but I think we might be able to fit in a campfire."

"Then we need marshmallows, chocolate bars and graham crackers." Eleanor pulled her cell phone from her purse and tapped out a message. "I asked Dot to pick some up."

Ruth finished gathering the items on her list and the women headed to the front of the store to wait for Dot and the others.

Gloria kept an eye on the grocery aisle. She spied Dot's hat as they rounded the corner. "No wonder it took them longer to shop. Check out the grocery cart."

Dot's cart was piled high. There were cases of bottled water and soda, bags of chips, boxes of snack crackers, loaves of bread and packages of buns and lunchmeat.

"Thanks for picking up the s'mores goodies." Eleanor pointed to a box of graham crackers teetering on top.

"I got those and a whole lot more," Dot said.

"You didn't stick to the list?" Ruth asked.

"We expanded the list and picked up some extra items," Rose said. "We have a lot of mouths to feed during the next couple of days."

Ruth led the way to the nearest checkout lane and unloaded her cart. After she finished unloading, Dot and Rose placed the food items on the belt.

Gloria attempted to tally the total and came up with a rough estimate. Even she wasn't prepared for the sticker shock.

"Your total is four hundred fifteen dollars and twelve cents," the cashier said.

Ruth calmly swiped her debit card and then entered her pin.

"We'll split the costs and pay you back," Gloria promised.

"We can divvy it up later," Ruth said as she took the receipt. "I figured we can fill the Styrofoam coolers with ice and then throw the refrigerator stuff inside before we head to our destination."

The women made quick work of unloading the shopping carts while Ruth filled the coolers with ice. Gloria followed behind, filling one cooler with sodas and bottled water while Dot filled the other with food.

Soon, they were on their way, but not for long. Ruth turned off the main road and sped past a sign too fast for Gloria to read it. "What did the sign say?"

"It said we'll be there in a minute," Ruth teased.

The road narrowed. Gloria's concern over their final destination grew as the area became sparsely populated and more rural.

"I'm afraid of bears." Rose gazed fearfully out the window. "It looks like we're heading into bear country."

"Or gators." Eleanor clapped her hands. "Ruth, you're a doll. I do believe I will get to see a gator after all. I've never seen a bear in the natural either. That would definitely be a bucket list worthy sighting."

An anxious hush fell over the van as the occupants sped down the road. There was another street sign. Gloria was only able to catch a glimpse and the word, "banks."

She started to ask Ruth what "banks" meant when Ruth veered into a gravel parking lot and abruptly stopped. "We're here."

Chapter 3

"Where is 'here?'" Margaret asked as she unbuckled her seatbelt.

"It's a boat ramp." Gloria frowned as she peered through the windshield.

"Yep," Ruth beamed. "And not just any boat ramp. It's the Gator House Landing boat ramp."

"We're going for a boat ride?" Dot asked.

"Sort of. I can't wait for you to see the surprise." Ruth stepped out of the van and waited for the others to join her before making her way along the dock to a small, wooden shack.

Gloria followed Ruth inside.

"Ruth Carpenter. I'm here to pick up my rental."

The man behind the desk slipped his reading glasses on. "Ms. Carpenter. Welcome to Gator

House Landing. I have some paperwork to go over and forms for you to sign."

"I'll wait outside." Gloria backed out of the shack and wandered along the dock, admiring several pontoon boats and speedboats as she walked. Her heart skipped a beat when she spied a couple of larger boats near the end.

Lucy caught up with Gloria and fell into step. "Do you see what I see?"

"Yes. If I'm not mistaken, those are houseboats."

"You don't think..." Lucy's voice trailed off.

"Wait up."

Gloria and Lucy slowed to let Eleanor catch up. "Look at the boats. Are those houseboats? Do you think we're renting a houseboat?"

A funny feeling in the pit of Gloria's stomach told her that was exactly what they were doing...renting a houseboat. She said the first thing that popped into her head. "Does Ruth know how to operate a houseboat?"

"I dunno. She won that speedboat on the gameshow *Dash for Cash* a while back," Lucy reminded them. "I'm sure she knows how to drive a boat, but a houseboat?"

"I hope so, because if not we may be sitting right here in the marina for the next few days."

Several loud voices echoed down the dock. Gloria watched as Ruth, followed by Rose, Dot and Margaret walked toward them, all talking over the top of each other.

"It's fine. It will be fine," Ruth assured them. "We'll have a blast. You need to relax."

Gloria could tell from the look on Ruth's face she was beginning to have second thoughts and jumped in to help her friend. "We need to give this a chance. I've never been on a houseboat. We might love it."

"We are going to the beach though, right?" Dot asked.

"Yes, we are staying at an oceanfront condo. Three nights on the houseboat, three nights on the ocean," Ruth said.

"That's a relief - although I could've used my dried marshmallow leaf potion on this trip." Rose sighed heavily. "What's done is done."

"Or you could be sitting in jail right now," Dot reminded her.

"Which houseboat is ours?" Lucy asked.

"The second one from the end. Someone just returned it. The agent told me they still need to clean it and gas it up, so we're gonna head to the Gator House Restaurant to grab a bite to eat. I have some discount coupons."

"Oh." Eleanor clasped her hands. "I wonder if they serve gator bites."

"I thought you wanted to see gators, not eat them," Margaret laughed.

The restaurant was river rustic, with worn clapboard siding and an open deck area overlooking the river. It reminded Gloria of a larger version of the rental shack.

They stepped inside and she pointed to a sign. "Seat yourself. I see a table over there, but it hasn't been cleared."

The women walked to the back and began clearing the few dishes when a man stormed across the dining room. "What are you doing?" he demanded.

"Clearing the table." Ruth barely gave him a glance. "There's nowhere else to sit."

"This is my table."

"I don't see your name on it." Ruth reached for a plate.

"I was in the bathroom." The man slid a chair out and plopped down, glaring at Ruth and daring her to say anything.

"I'm sorry. We had no idea," Gloria said. "We thought the table was empty."

"Well think again."

A young woman hurried over. "I thought you left, Larry, or I would've stopped these ladies." She finished clearing the table and apologized for the confusion.

"It's okay. We're staying right here." Ruth motioned to the others after the young woman carried the tray of dishes away. "Have a seat."

Gloria reluctantly perched on the edge of a chair, painfully aware of the man's angry glare. The others joined her and they began discussing their houseboat plans.

Larry cleared his throat and shoved his chair back. "I can't take another second of your mindless chatter." He marched to the exit, but not before threatening them that they would be sorry for messing with Larry Molson.

"Good riddance," Ruth muttered.

The server returned to the table carrying a tray of ice waters. "Larry is a regular and this is his favorite table."

"It's not your fault…"

"Darcy. I'm sorry. My name is Darcy and I'll be taking care of you today."

"Darcy," Gloria repeated. "Maybe Larry is having a bad day."

"He has a bad day every day." She set the glasses on the table before pulling a notepad from her pocket. "Can I get you something other than ice waters?"

The women ordered sodas and after Darcy left, Ruth went over the details of the houseboat rental.

Gloria, realizing there was nothing to do but accept the fact they were staying on a houseboat, forced herself to focus on the bright side. They would only be on the houseboat for a couple of days. "Think of how peaceful and relaxing it will be."

"Full of mosquitoes and bugs, not to mention slithering critters," Margaret griped. "What in the world possessed you to book a houseboat, Ruth?"

"I got a good deal on it. Eleanor was the one who gave me the idea. She kept talking about seeing gators and I thought why spend our entire vacation on a crowded beach with a bunch of other tourists?"

"We *are* the tourists," Lucy pointed out. "I guess I can see your point, Ruth. Why not see the real Florida?"

"I think it's an excellent idea." Eleanor's eyes shined. "I've never been on a houseboat before."

"Neither have I," Gloria said. "From what little I saw, it looks nice."

"I rented the biggest one available, although we'll have to share a bunkhouse."

"That's fine with me," Dot said. "Thank you for picking such a...unique vacation."

Darcy returned with their sodas. The women each ordered a sandwich, except for Eleanor, who was thrilled when she found out the restaurant served deep fried gator bites. She ordered the gator bites, along with a side of coleslaw and hushpuppies.

When the food arrived, Eleanor offered each of them a taste of the gator. They all politely declined except for Dot, who sampled a small piece, claiming it tasted like fried chicken.

Eleanor popped the last morsel in her mouth and dabbed at the corner of her lips with her napkin. "The gator bites were delicious. You don't know what you're missing."

"We'll take your word for it," Lucy said.

Ruth guzzled the last of her soda and glanced at her watch. "The houseboat should be ready."

They each paid for their food and Ruth returned to the small office to pick up the keys. She followed the man to the houseboat and the others trailed behind, anxious to check out their accommodations.

From the outside, the houseboat appeared roomy. It sported a large open deck area. Gloria spotted a bucket of fishing poles and a box of fishing tackle. It reminded her of her husband, Paul. "This would be Paul's dream vacation."

"Ray and Johnnie's, too," Dot said.

The hot Florida sun beat down on them and beads of sweat soaked the side of Gloria's face as she waited for the marina employee to explain everything to Ruth. "I'm ready for some air conditioning."

Ruth and the man emerged and joined them on the dock. He handed her the keys and a plastic tote. "I have one final word of advice - keep an eye on the gas gauge. There are only a few places here on the river where you can get gas."

"Will do." Ruth gave the man a mock salute and waited until he was gone. "It's time to get this baby loaded and on the river."

"What's that?" Gloria pointed to the plastic tote.

"It's a box of goodies the rental company loans to guests, so they don't have to pack a bunch of unnecessary stuff."

"You mean like the stuff we just purchased at the store?" Lucy joshed.

"No." Ruth lifted her chin. "Did you see me buying rubber gloves, a set of screwdrivers and garbage bags at the store?"

"I was kidding." Lucy grabbed the tote. "I'll put this inside the houseboat if you want to start unloading the van."

The women loaded the luggage first. They returned to the van a second time to gather the bags of groceries and the coolers. After their third and final trip, Gloria was ready for a nap. She cast a longing look toward the shoreline, wondering if they would regret the river adventure.

"Do you mind if I hang out with you?" Eleanor followed Ruth upstairs while Gloria explored the main level, thanking the Good Lord they weren't camping in a tent.

The kitchen was small, but well equipped. A long bar with barstools separated the kitchen area from the living room.

Along both sides of the living room were comfy sofas. A narrow hall and a set of doors were beyond the kitchen. Behind one door was a toilet and sink and on the other side of the hall, a shower.

Near the back was the sleeping area - the bunkhouse - with enough bunks to sleep six people.

Gloria was still inspecting the bunks when Eleanor plodded down the spiral staircase. "What's upstairs?"

"Lots of nifty stuff. You should check it out. Ruth is still up there."

35

Ruth stood at the top of the stairwell and motioned to Gloria. "C'mon up."

Gloria reluctantly climbed the spiral stairs. By the time she reached the top, she felt lightheaded. "I won't be doing that often."

"Well?" Ruth beamed. "Eleanor and I nicknamed this the crow's nest. What do you think?"

The small room was sparsely furnished. In one corner was a narrow cot. A wooden dresser was in the opposite corner. To the left was a slider.

"It's cozy. What's out there?" Gloria pointed to a smaller, open deck.

"There's another set of navigational controls. It's what they call the flybridge."

"You steer the boat from up here?" Gloria asked.

"Yes. There's a navigational system downstairs, too. I think I like this better. Check out the view." Ruth opened the sliders and Gloria stuck her head out.

The upper deck sported an unobstructed view of the marina and the river. "I think you should take the cot up here since you'll be the one navigating the boat."

Ruth cast an uneasy glance toward the spiral staircase, where the sound of excited chatter drifted up. "I don't think the others are thrilled with my surprise."

"I'll be the first to admit I was shocked when I realized you rented a houseboat," Gloria said. "I'm starting to get used to the idea. The weather is gorgeous, the sun is shining and we're here with our best friends. What more could we want?"

"You're right." Ruth appeared visibly relieved. "I almost cancelled the reservation when it dawned on me I would be the one responsible for driving the houseboat. It was too late by the time I had second thoughts. We would've lost our deposit, so I snuck over to a small marina near Green Springs a coupla weeks ago to practice. It was tricky, but I figured it out."

"Hey, you guys." Lucy appeared in the stairwell. "We have something for Ruth."

"We're on our way down." Gloria kept a tight grip on the railing as she followed Ruth to the main deck.

When they reached the bottom, Eleanor presented Ruth with a captain's hat. "I found this in the closet. You're not the official captain until you put the hat on."

Ruth promptly placed the hat on her head. "It fits."

"Of course it does," Gloria said. "Let's take some pictures."

The women gathered on the open deck and posed for several pictures.

"It's time to get this baby on the river before it gets dark," Ruth said.

"Aye-aye, captain." Gloria eased onto an empty bench seat and breathed deeply as she gazed out at the open water.

"Hey!" A familiar male voice echoed across the marina, causing the hair on the back of Gloria's neck to go up. "Are you nitwits gonna lollygag all day?"

Larry, the man that the women confronted inside the restaurant, stood on the dock, glaring at Gloria. She prayed Ruth hadn't heard, but it was too late.

Her friend stomped out onto the open deck and placed her hands on her hips. "What are you whining about now, jerk?"

"Your piece of crap rental is bumping into my houseboat." He jabbed his finger at the sporty, sleek houseboat tied up directly behind them.

"Then move," Ruth shrugged. "Problem solved."

Two men joined Larry on the dock. "Let 'em be." One of them said as they placed a light hand on Larry's shoulder.

Larry jerked his arm away and took a menacing step towards them.

"Let's go," Gloria said quietly.

Ruth gave Larry and his companions a hard stare before storming inside and slamming the slider door.

Lucy tossed the ropes on board the houseboat and joined Gloria on the open deck.

She cast an uneasy glance toward the slider, praying her friend would calm down enough to maneuver the houseboat out of the marina and into open waters.

The water began to churn and the houseboat began to float away from the dock, right before Gloria heard a loud *thunk* and they shuddered to a halt.

Chapter 4

"You hit my boat." Larry strode to the edge of the dock.

For a minute, Gloria briefly thought he was going to jump onto their houseboat.

Ruth must have thought the same. She gunned the motor. The houseboat made a loud grinding noise as it lurched to the side.

The man began to cuss, as the grinding grew louder.

Gloria squeezed her eyes shut, bracing for the full effects of Larry's wrath. When she opened them, the boat was a safe distance away from the dock and Larry.

"We did it." Eleanor clapped. "Good-bye, Larry the bully!"

He gave them the finger. Gloria could see his lips moving, and was glad she couldn't hear what he was saying.

Ruth returned the one finger salute.

"Ruth," Gloria chided.

"He's starting to tick me off."

"What if he turns us in to the marina for damaging his boat?"

"Big deal. I bought the extra rental insurance, just in case."

Gloria started to ask how much the extra insurance cost them, but decided she didn't want to know, at least not yet.

With the ordeal behind them, they coasted along the St. Johns River. The others joined Gloria and they scanned the waters and shoreline for gators and other wildlife.

Lucy pointed out several white pelicans and a flock of ducks while Eleanor insisted she spotted a set of beady alligator eyes off in the distance.

Gloria motioned to Ruth, who was in front of the flybridge controls. "Where are we staying tonight?"

"I found a small marina not far from here." Ruth glanced at her watch. "We should start heading there now. Since I'm not familiar with the river, I want to dock and get settled in before dark."

Ruth explained the marina was the perfect spot and not far from some springs she wanted to scope out the following day.

Determined to avoid another houseboat collision, Margaret and Rose stationed themselves near the front and helped guide the vessel through the narrow channel.

Thankfully, there were several open slips near the end of the marina and close to the river. It took Ruth a couple of attempts before she was able to steer the houseboat into one of the spots.

Lucy donned a pair of work gloves she found in the borrowed tote and joined Margaret and Rose near the front. "While we were riding, I watched a video on my phone on how to tie up to the dock."

"I know how to tie up the boat." Ruth joined them, wearing her own set of gloves. "We need to tie up the bow and stern and spring lines."

"Don't forget the plastic thingies to make sure the boat doesn't bump the dock," Lucy said.

"The boat fenders. I already put them on." Ruth stepped onto the dock and began tying up the bow of the boat.

Lucy made her way to the other end and began tying up the stern. "I'm using a cleat hitch. It's one of the more popular knots used by boaters." Her face contorted as she attempted to tie the knot. "It's not as easy as the video made it seem."

"Here, let me help." Ruth had already tied up her end and joined Lucy in the back.

"You made that look easy," Lucy said.

"I've been practicing." Ruth tugged the gloves off and shoved them in her back pocket.

"You didn't ding the boat, did you?" Gloria pointed to a section of missing dock a stone's throw from their houseboat.

"No, I did not," Ruth said. "I barely nicked Larry's houseboat and he better not try to sue us."

"I wouldn't bet on it," Lucy said. "He was pretty ticked off."

"Yeah, well he didn't have to act like such a jerk." Ruth changed the subject. "Remind me later that I need to stop by the office to let them know we're here."

"Do you have any idea what the charge will be to spend the night?" Gloria was beginning to wonder how much all of the extra expenses would cost... the houseboat rental, gas, the extra insurance and now dock space.

"Their rates are reasonable," Ruth shrugged. "If you're worried about the cost, I'll pay for it myself."

Feeling like a cheapskate, Gloria shook her head. "I can pay my share. I'm just curious."

"I think it's like a hundred dollars for the night. It includes electric hookup and water. Not a bad deal for seven people."

Except they'd already spent several hundred dollars renting the houseboat. But Gloria didn't mention that. Split seven ways it wasn't much money, plus they were saving money by not eating out, so Gloria couldn't complain. "You're right. It's a bargain."

The friends crowded into the bunkhouse to determine who was going to sleep where, all voting for Ruth to get the crow's nest.

"I have another special surprise planned for tomorrow," Ruth said.

"Another surprise?" Margaret asked. "I'm not ready for another surprise."

"You'll like it. Trust me." Ruth patted her stomach. "I'm starving. After we eat, I'm going to run up to the marina office."

Dinner consisted of lunchmeat sandwiches and chips. While they ate, the women chatted about their plans for the following day, each trying to guess what Ruth's "special surprise" might be. Ruth insisted none of them was even close.

"I better head to the office to check in and pay for our night's stay before the office closes." Ruth grabbed her purse and stepped outside.

"I'll tag along." Gloria caught up with Ruth and they began making their way to the marina office. "The plan is to spend the night here and then head out in the morning for some sightseeing?"

"Yes. We'll be leaving sometime tomorrow morning, but not early."

"We have to wait for the surprise?" Gloria hinted.

"No, at least not here. You'll see." Ruth grinned. "I recognize the look on your face and not knowing is driving you crazy. Remember, good things come to those who wait."

"Hmm." Gloria wasn't convinced and remained silent for the rest of the walk as she mulled over Ruth's surprise.

She followed her friend into the marina office, a small and dreary space. An unpleasant odor emanated from the room. Gloria clamped her hand across her nose. "Yuck."

The heavyset man standing behind the counter snorted. "Ya don't care for the smell of our stink bait?"

"Stink is right," Ruth gasped. "It smells like something decomposing."

"Close." The man shoved his chubby hand into the jar next to him and grabbed a handful of what appeared to be gummy worms.

He tilted his head back and dangled one over his open mouth before dropping it in. "It's our own special catfish bait, a mixture of shad, a fancy name for fish food and a tub of chicken livers. I mix 'em up in a bucket and then set the bucket in the sun until it turns to mush."

Gloria felt her stomach grow queasy as she watched the man chomp away on his catfish bait.

Ruth leaned her elbow on the counter and eyed him with interest. "Decomposing chicken livers would definitely smell."

"Yep." The man nodded. "Could also be the limburger cheese mixed in. If you can get past the chicken livers, it doesn't taste too bad. I just made a fresh batch, which is what you smell. You want to try some?"

Gloria's eyes widened as her stomach threatened to heave. "No...thank you. I'll pass."

"Maybe next time. I'm not keen on food poisoning." Ruth pointed at the jar. "Rotting fish and chicken livers sitting in the hot sun all day? No thanks."

The man cracked a smile, exposing a toothless grin. "Did you gals think I was eating catfish bait?" He tapped his hand on top of the jar. "These are gummy worms. The catfish bait is in this jar." He reached under the counter and pulled out a glass jar, filled with pale yellow cubes floating in a thick liquid. "This here is the catfish bait."

"Our friend, Rose, might be interested in your catfish bait," Gloria said. "She likes unusual concoctions."

"My bait has been selling like hotcakes. I'll be closing the office soon and we don't open up again until six tomorrow morning. If your friend is interested and I'm not around, tell her to ask for Buddy's special stink bait."

"You're Buddy?" Gloria asked.

"Yep."

"I'll let her know."

"The reason we're here is to pay for a slip." Ruth set her purse on the counter. "Our houseboat is parked in slip number sixteen."

"Only one night?"

"Yes. We're leaving sometime tomorrow morning."

"We rent slips by reservation only and we're booked solid."

"I made a reservation," Ruth said. "It's under the name Ruth Carpenter."

Buddy flipped open a binder. "I found it. What size watercraft you got?"

"I don't know right off hand. I think it's around sixty feet long. We rented the houseboat from the Gator House Landing."

"You rented it from Roy Paver." The man gave them an odd look, but it quickly vanished. "Roy's only got a coupla houseboats. What color is it?"

"Blue and white."

"It's his sixty footer." Buddy slipped his reading glasses on. "We charge a buck seventy five per foot. Your sixty footer is gonna be a hundred and five dollars for the night."

"A hundred and five dollars," Gloria croaked. "Just to dock our houseboat for less than twenty-four hours?"

Buddy frowned. "The fee includes water and electric." He drummed his fingers on the counter. "Tell you what...I like you two and I kinda feel bad about tricking you into thinking I was eating catfish bait." He cackled loudly as he gazed at Gloria. "Young lady, your face was green as the grass."

He continued. "So I'm gonna give you a five dollar discount and make it an even hundred for the night."

"Perfect." Ruth handed him her credit card.

"We charge an extra five percent for credit card charges." Buddy placed the card on an old credit card slider and slid the bar across the top. He handed Ruth's card to her and reached for a pen to fill in the charges.

"So we're back to a hundred and five," Gloria said.

"Yep. It's better than a hundred and ten." Buddy passed the pen to Ruth to sign the receipt before ripping off the top part and handing it to her. "Don't forget to tell your friend about the catfish bait."

"We will. Are you the owner of the marina, Buddy?"

"Nope. The owners are Fitz and Caroline Buchanan. They're off for the rest of the day. You'll meet them tomorrow morning. Can't miss Fitz. He's about seven foot tall, skinny as a rail and as bald as a cue ball."

"I see," Gloria said. "Thanks for the information and we'll be sure to tell our friend about your catfish bait."

"Like I said, I'm getting ready to close, but we open again tomorrow morning at six."

Gloria thanked Buddy for the information and the women exited the store. Ruth pulled the door shut behind them. "Buddy is a character."

"No kidding. I almost lost my cookies when I thought he was eating rotting fish and chicken livers." Gloria made a gagging sound.

"Me too," Ruth wrinkled her nose. "I'm sorry the houseboat is turning into a money pit."

"It's okay." Gloria patted Ruth's shoulder. "Like you said, we're going to split the costs. Less than twenty bucks each is a bargain."

When they reached the houseboat, they found Eleanor up in the crow's nest, leaning over the railing, cell phone in hand.

"What are you doing?" Gloria hollered.

"I'm taking pictures. I could've sworn I saw a gator swimming out behind the houseboat." Eleanor scrambled down the ladder and hopped onto the lower deck. "His eyes were big and beady and he kept swimming back and forth."

"I'm surprised you didn't head to a lower deck to get a closer look," Ruth said.

"I did, but every time I got close he disappeared." Eleanor waved her phone. "I got some great pictures of the marina while I was up there. I love the houseboat, Ruth. What a great idea."

"Thanks," Ruth beamed. "I'm glad you're enjoying it."

The excitement of the day was beginning to catch up with Gloria. She lifted both hands over her head. "I'm whupped. I think I'm going to call it a day."

"Me too," Eleanor said. "I want to be up early to try to look for gators before we leave."

The women took turns in the bathroom before settling into their bunks. Gloria was the last to head to bed. The air inside the bunkroom was musty and damp. She turned the a/c unit on high and crawled under the scratchy blankets.

Before drifting off to sleep, she thanked God for time with her friends, for arriving at the marina safely and prayed for a relaxing, restful vacation.

Gloria woke early the next morning to bright sunlight pouring into the bunkhouse through a gap in the window shades. After tossing and turning, she finally gave up on going back to sleep. She threw the covers off and tiptoed out of the room.

She found Ruth seated at the bar, poring over a map. The tantalizing aroma of freshly brewed coffee filled the cabin.

"You're up early." Gloria poured a cup and joined Ruth at the bar. "Whatcha got?"

"It's a river map. I'm planning our day." Ruth turned her attention to Gloria. "How did you sleep?"

"Like a baby. Yesterday was long and traveling always stresses me out."

"Me, too." Ruth folded the map and slid it off to the side. "It didn't help having Larry the bully harass us. I barely nicked the side of his houseboat. A hundred bucks says I didn't even leave a scratch."

"Hopefully, that's the last we see of Larry." Gloria glanced out the window. "I bet it's nice outside."

"Nice and peaceful," Ruth said. "I love early mornings when it's quiet."

Gloria and Ruth refilled their coffee cups and wandered out onto the open deck. The small marina was full of pontoons, speedboats and cabin cruisers. Parked next to them was another houseboat.

"Another houseboat pulled in last night." Gloria wandered to the railing and something caught her eye. "Ruth, do you see that?"

"I sure do. The houseboat next to us looks like the bully's houseboat."

"It does. How did we get so lucky?" Gloria groaned.

"He didn't tie his boat up right and now it's drifting into our space." Ruth leaned over the side.

She stretched out her hand, her fingertips nearly touching the rear corner of the other houseboat.

Ruth jerked upright, making a gurgling sound. "You're not gonna believe this."

"Not gonna believe what?" Gloria set her coffee cup on the table and peered into the murky water. "What am I looking at?"

"Over there." Ruth pointed. "Near the edge of the dock."

Gloria's eyes grew wide. She said the first thing that popped into her head. "It looks like I just lost my bet with Paul."

Chapter 5

"Quick! We need to do something." Gloria kicked off her shoes, ready to dive in and rescue the person who was floating face down, mere inches from the side of their houseboat.

"I'm going in," Ruth said. "You call for help."

Before Gloria could reply, Ruth jumped over the side and began treading water.

Gloria darted back inside the houseboat and to the kitchen counter where she'd left her cell phone charging. Her fingers trembled as she dialed 911.

"911. What's your emergency?"

"Yes. My name is Gloria Kennedy. I'm at a marina on the St. Johns River and there's a body in the water, floating face down. My friend jumped in to try to rescue him."

"What marina, ma'am?"

Gloria's mind drew a blank. "I don't know. We pulled in late last night. I have no idea." She ran out of the houseboat and onto the dock before racing to the marina office. "It's the *Sunshine Bridge Marina.*"

"And exactly where is the body?"

"Floating next to our houseboat. Hang on." Gloria hustled back to the houseboat, frantically searching for a slip number. "I can't find the slip number. My friend is trying to pull the person from the water."

"Gloria," Ruth gasped, "I need some help." Her friend reached one of the piers, struggling to stay afloat with one arm wrapped around the man's shoulders.

"We have a unit on the way."

"I gotta go." Gloria disconnected the line and tossed the phone on the bench seat before dropping to her knees.

60

"I'll try to push him closer." Ruth flailed around as she attempted to nudge the person closer to the dock.

"That's it." Gloria lunged forward and clawed at the man's flannel shirt. She held tight after grabbing a fistful of material and then wiggled backward, pulling him along with her.

Ruth paddled backwards to assess the situation. "There's no way the two of us are going to be able to lift him out of the water. He's too heavy."

"Maybe if you can give me one of his arms," Gloria grunted.

"I can't. His hands are tied behind his back. Besides...it's too late. He's a goner."

The sound of sirens off in the distance drew closer. "The cops are coming."

"What's going on?" Lucy stepped onto the open deck. "You couldn't wait to go fishing?"

"Not quite. Can you give Ruth a hand up?" Gloria asked.

"Sure, but what is Ruth doing in the water?"

Ruth planted the bottom of her shoe on the post as Lucy wrapped both hands around her friend's arm and pulled.

"Why are you swimming in the marina?"

"We're not swimming," Gloria said. "I'm holding onto a body."

"You're kidding." Lucy peered over the edge. "No, you're not kidding."

"We found him floating face down near the back of the houseboat. Gloria already called 911. I think he's dead. He's too heavy for us to lift him out."

"I'll run to the marina store to get help." Lucy scrambled to her feet and jogged down the dock.

"Ruth, I think this is Larry." Gloria adjusted her grip. "That's his houseboat. I'm pretty sure he was wearing this flannel shirt yesterday."

"You're right." Droplets of water splattered on the deck as Ruth wrung out her t-shirt. "I remember thinking he was crazy for wearing a long-sleeved flannel shirt in this Florida heat. This doesn't look good."

"If this is Larry, there were witnesses who watched you hit his houseboat, right before you gave him the one finger salute."

"Yeah, well he did it first."

"It doesn't make him any less dead," Gloria pointed out. "I think it's in our best interest to take a couple of pictures before the police get here."

Before Ruth could reply, the rest of the women, hearing the commotion outside, joined them.

Dot's eyes grew round as saucers. "What happened?"

"Ruth found a body by the boat. She jumped in to try to rescue the person and we discovered not only is the person dead, it's Larry."

63

"Larry?" Margaret shook her head.

"Larry, the man we had a run in with at the other marina, who freaked out when I nicked the side of his houseboat," Ruth said.

Eleanor cautiously approached Gloria and peered over the side of the boat. "Sure enough. It's a body."

"What can we do to help?" Dot joined Eleanor.

"Nothing," Gloria said. "I called the cops. Lucy ran to the office for help."

The sound of the sirens grew louder.

"On second thought, there is something you can do. We need to take a few pictures, and we better do it quick," Gloria urged.

"I've got my cell phone." Margaret waved her cell phone in the air.

"Start snapping pictures of everything."

Margaret snapped several pictures of the dock, Larry's houseboat, the distance between the houseboats and finally a couple shots of Gloria, who was still holding onto the back of what she now believed was Larry Molson's flannel shirt.

Whoop. Gloria caught a glimpse of two police cars as they careened into the marina parking lot. They stopped in front of the office. "Maybe the rest of you should wait inside."

"I agree." Dot returned indoors. Rose and Margaret followed behind.

Eleanor hesitated. "Can I stay?"

"You better go, too." Gloria watched Eleanor reluctantly make her way back inside. She could see her standing on the other side of the slider, peering out.

Lucy, followed by two uniformed police officers and a tall, thin man Gloria guessed was the marina owner, along with a petite gray-haired woman, hurried to the houseboat.

One of the officers kicked off his shoes. He handed his gun to his partner and jumped in the water. "I'll take over."

Gloria released her grip before shifting to her knees. She reached behind her and massaged the cramp in her lower back before limping across the deck to join her friends.

Everything moved fast after that, as more officers and firetrucks arrived, along with divers. It took several attempts for the divers, assisted by a trio of police officers, to pull the man's body from the water.

An ambulance arrived on scene. After a quick examination of the victim, they eased him onto a stretcher, covered his body with a sheet and then loaded the stretcher into the back of the ambulance.

"It's time to secure the crime scene." One of the officers, the one Gloria guessed was in charge, nodded toward a group of gawkers, gathered nearby.

"Yes, sir." A younger male officer motioned to the onlookers. "Step back folks."

An officer approached Ruth, Lucy and Gloria. "Who found the body?"

"We did." Ruth pointed to Gloria. "I noticed the houseboat next to us was tied at an odd angle. I made a comment to my friend that I wondered how we were going to get out with the other boat so close to ours."

The officer pulled a notepad from his pocket and flipped it open. "Do you know approximately what time you first noticed the victim in the water?"

"It was around six-thirty," Gloria said. "I remember looking at the clock and thinking it was awfully bright outside for six-thirty."

"Yes," Ruth agreed. "It was around six-thirty."

The officer began scribbling in his notepad. "Do you recall noticing anyone in the vicinity, perhaps on the dock or in the houseboat next door?"

The women both told him 'no.' He then asked them if they heard any unusual noises during the night, screaming or a commotion that may have indicated an argument.

"No," Gloria shook her head. "I didn't hear a thing. We had the window air conditioning unit turned on."

"Me either," Ruth said.

The officer pointed to Lucy. "Do you have anything to add?"

"No. I came out after my friends found the poor man's body."

"Is it just the three of you?"

"We have four more friends. They're inside," Gloria said. "We thought it best if they stayed out of the way."

"I would like to talk to them."

Ruth led the man inside. Lucy waited until the door closed behind them. "This is terrible. Do you know how bad this looks?"

"Pretty bad," Gloria admitted. "Do you think this Larry person followed us to the marina with plans to stir up trouble?"

"I can't imagine the chances of him happening to be at this marina the same night we're here and just happening to be docked right next to us." Lucy began to pace. "He seemed a little unbalanced. I think I remember seeing a couple of other guys with him yesterday when he was yelling at us on the dock. What if Larry was murdered and his killer is here, watching us?"

Gloria glanced at the group of bystanders nearby. "Honestly, after Ruth clipped Larry's houseboat, we were in such a hurry to get out of there, all I wanted to do was put as much distance as possible between him and us."

"Me, too. Looking back, I wish we had."

The officer, accompanied by Ruth, exited the houseboat. "Ruth mentioned that all of you are from out-of-state. I'm guessing you didn't know the victim."

Ruth and Gloria exchanged a quick glance. The officer's sharp eye caught the exchange. "You knew the victim?"

"Not...technically," Ruth blurted out. "We ran into the owner of the other houseboat yesterday while we were leaving the Gator House Landing."

"Literally," Gloria mumbled.

"What did you say?"

"We were involved in a minor run-in with the man inside the Gator House Restaurant and then again when we were leaving the landing," Gloria said. "We accidentally bumped his boat and he yelled at us."

"I see." The officer motioned to another officer. They shifted off to the side and began talking in low voices.

"Why did you tell him that?" Ruth hissed.

"Because he was going to find out. I don't want it to look like we were trying to withhold information," Gloria whispered back. "We're innocent. We have plenty of witnesses to back us up."

Before Ruth could reply, the investigating officer made his way back over.

Gloria had a sudden thought. "I would like to point out there were two men at the other marina, standing on the dock with Mr. Molson when we were leaving. We have no idea who they were."

The officer jotted a few more notes and flipped the notepad shut. "I'll need a copy of each of your driver's licenses or photo identification. Because this is being investigated as a suspicious death, you're not allowed to leave the area until authorized to do so."

"Can we leave this marina?" Ruth asked. "We planned on leaving today." She told the officer they were renting the houseboat for a couple more days and then planned to head to an oceanfront resort.

"You can leave the marina, but not the state. I'll be reaching out to you again later today or tomorrow. Before I leave, I would like your permission to have a look around your houseboat."

"Of course." Ruth opened the slider. "Eleanor will show you around."

Gloria watched as other officers finished inspecting Larry's houseboat. They exited onto the dock and approached the couple standing near the police tape. Occasionally, one of them would motion in their direction.

The lead investigator exited the houseboat with Eleanor trailing behind. He gave the women a curt nod and joined the others before they slowly made their way to the marina office. Finally, the officers and the investigators climbed into their cars and drove off.

"What a mess." Gloria flopped down on the bench seat. She gazed somberly at Larry Molson's houseboat, regretting ever crossing paths with the man. "Someone murdered Larry. If his actions towards us yesterday are any indication of how he treats others, I'm certain he had at least a couple of enemies."

She tried to remember what the other men, who were standing with Larry on the dock, looked like. Gloria turned to Ruth. "Do you remember the name of the young girl who waited on us at the Gator House Restaurant yesterday?"

"Marcy?" Lucy guessed.

"Her name was Darcy," Eleanor said. "Darcy is my niece's name."

"I think we need to stop back by the Gator House and ask a few questions of our own," Gloria said. "Remember how Darcy said Larry was giving her a hard time? There's a good chance she knows the names of the two men who were with Larry when he was yelling at us."

"You're right," Ruth said. "We need to start our own investigation."

"We need to do a little digging around here, at the marina." Gloria abruptly stood. "I'm sure the tall guy, standing on the dock and the petite woman were the owners. The man fit the description Buddy gave us yesterday." She turned to Ruth. "Fitz something."

"Fitz and Caroline. I don't remember the last name. I'm sure you're right. Buddy described Fitz as tall and bald as a cue ball. I doubt they'll talk to us since we're suspects." Ruth slowly turned, eyeing the other friends who had remained inside during the police investigation. "Dot…"

Dot's eyes grew wide. "What?" she squeaked. "You know I'm a wimp and terrible at investigating. I'll choke."

"Oh brother." Ruth rolled her eyes. "What about you, Rose?"

"No," Gloria interrupted. "We may need to use Rose later."

Ruth and Gloria turned to Margaret.

74

"Fine," Margaret briefly closed her eyes. "I have no problem doing a little intel."

"That's the spirit." Gloria clapped her hands.

"It's either that, or we can wait for the cops to track us down and throw Ruth in the slammer. At the very least, we'll end up stuck on this houseboat for who knows how long until the authorities let us leave the state."

"I'll go with you." Eleanor, who had been as quiet as a church mouse, spoke.

"Are you sure?" Gloria asked.

"Positive. The marina owners didn't see me." Eleanor pointed to Margaret. "Or Margaret. In fact, while all of you were chit chatting about the death, I was thinking to myself, 'Eleanor Whittaker, this is the perfect opportunity to prove yourself worthy of being a Garden Girl's super sleuth.'"

"We need a plan," Ruth said bluntly. "But first, I want to get out of here."

"Oh, I have a plan," Eleanor's eyes twinkled with mischief. She tapped the side of her forehead. "It may not look like I'm paying attention, but I watch you girls like a hawk. I think I might have a trick or two of my own up my sleeve."

Chapter 6

"I'm not sure about this." Ruth waited until Lucy finished tying the houseboat up at the Gator House Landing before holding out the keys to the rental van. "If anything happens to this van, my butt is on the line."

"If you're concerned about the rental van, Ruth, why don't you drive Eleanor and Margaret back to the other marina?" Gloria suggested. "The rest of us can wait here, on the houseboat until you get back."

"You'll be gone an hour, hour and a half tops," Lucy chimed in.

"I don't understand why we left," Ruth grumbled. "We were already *at* the Sunshine Bridge Marina."

"We need to pretend that we're new customers," Eleanor patiently explained. "Which is why we need to arrive via vehicle."

"Fine. I'll drive you *back* to the marina we just left." Ruth jabbed her finger at Gloria. "I'm putting you in charge of the houseboat. Don't let anything happen to it."

"You mean like colliding with another houseboat and leaving a long scrape along the side?" Gloria teased.

Ruth scowled. "I didn't do it on purpose and I wish I'd never laid eyes on Larry Molson."

"You aren't the only one," Margaret grunted.

"We'll stay right here," Dot promised.

"It's a shame Darcy, the server at the Gator House Restaurant, isn't working," Lucy said. "We could talk to her while Margaret and Eleanor chat with the owners of the other marina."

"It might work out better this way." Gloria gazed at Eleanor thoughtfully. "You two gather as much information as possible from the employees at the other marina, and then we'll see what clues we can glean here."

"Well, we better snap to it." Ruth headed toward the parking lot.

"Wait!" Eleanor darted down the dock and disappeared inside the houseboat.

"Maybe I should've gone by myself," Margaret said.

"And burst Eleanor's bubble?" Gloria asked. "Don't you see how excited she is?"

A vision of blue floated out of the houseboat and Eleanor glided towards them.

Gloria did a double take. "Eleanor?"

"Yes?" Bright blue eyes peered out from behind the wire-rimmed glasses.

"What are you wearing?" Dot asked.

"My housecoat."

Gloria chuckled. "Your housecoat?"

"Not just any housecoat...it's my lucky housecoat. I figured we were probably going to end up involved in some sort of calamity and I wanted to be prepared. Besides, it didn't take up much room in my suitcase."

"Yeah, who doesn't trust little old ladies?" Lucy laughed.

"Precisely." Eleanor shifted her patent leather bag to her other hand. "I've got a few goodies in my purse, if needed."

"A gun," Dot guessed.

"Nope. No gun," Eleanor said. "The TSA doesn't allow them in carry-ons."

"And you thought my potions were gonna get us in trouble," Rose said. "Eleanor, you are a handful."

"Times a wastin'." Ruth jangled the van keys. "No more chatting. It's time for action." She climbed behind the wheel of the van. Eleanor slid into the passenger seat while Margaret made her way to the back.

Gloria watched the van pull out of the marina parking lot and disappear from sight. "Well?"

"Eleanor seems convinced she can extract valuable information about Larry from the marina employees or owners," Lucy shrugged. "We were dead in the water since the owners got a good look at the two of us and Ruth."

"Ruth knows enough to stay out of sight," Dot said.

"Yep, and Margaret will do all right," Gloria said. "But Eleanor? She's the wild card."

Rose snorted. "You got that right. I have no idea what Eleanor's plan is."

"I'm sure we'll find out soon enough."

*****

A plume of dust trailed behind the van as Ruth circled the Sunshine Bridge Marina parking lot for the second time.

"Why don't you park right there?" Margaret jabbed her finger at an empty parking spot, not far from the marina office.

"Because I can't risk the owners seeing me in the van." Ruth crept between two boat trailers as she began her third spin around the parking lot.

"If you keep circling the lot, they're going to get suspicious."

"I see a spot over there, near the restrooms," Eleanor said.

"That'll work." Ruth stepped on the gas, a little too hard and a spray of gravel flew out from the rear tires of the van.

"Easy, speedy," Margaret cautioned.

Ruth ignored the comment as she eased the rental van into the parking spot. "Are you sure you're up for this?"

"Positive. I know exactly what I'm going to say." Eleanor turned to Margaret, seated directly behind her. "Follow my lead."

"I dunno. What if they get suspicious?"

"You don't question women my age. If we're not out in fifteen minutes, call the cops."

"Call the cops?" Ruth sputtered.

"Not really. I always wanted to say that because it sounds dangerous." Eleanor flung the door open and hopped out of the van.

"Careful with the acrobats," Ruth hollered. "You're supposed to be a fragile elderly woman."

"Right." Eleanor hunched her back and began shuffling toward the restrooms. She opened the door marked "women."

"These are the restrooms," Margaret whispered.

"I know. I gotta go," Eleanor whispered back. "Whenever I get over-excited I gotta go." She wandered into the nearest stall and closed the door behind her. "Hang onto my purse."

Eleanor's purse sailed over the top of the stall door and Margaret lunged forward to catch it. "Umpf."

While she waited, Margaret paced, a feeling of impending doom settling over her.

"I'm sad about Larry's death, but this is so exciting." Eleanor began to hum. "Don't you think it's exciting?"

"Yes, it's definitely out of the norm for my usual vacations," Margaret agreed. "Of course, we are vacationing with Gloria, so I guess I shouldn't be surprised."

The toilet flushed and Eleanor emerged from the stall. She wandered over to the sink and began washing her hands.

After drying them, Margaret handed her the purse.

"I was bluffing earlier. I'm scared witless."

"Scared of what?" Margaret opened the door and waited for Eleanor to step onto the sidewalk.

"That I'm going to mess up the investigation."

"Technically, there isn't an investigation, so there's nothing to mess up."

"Yes, but there will be." Eleanor cleared her throat. "I feel the weight of the world on my shoulders. If I mess up, Gloria will never trust me again."

"Yes, she will. What matters most is that you're trying. Now let's see if we can find out a little more about Larry Molson."

"Not yet," Eleanor grabbed Margaret's arm. "I think we should take a look around the marina first."

The women slowly walked along the pier, until they reached the spot where Molson's houseboat was docked. A line of yellow police tape still surrounded the dock area. Another boat, this one a speedboat, was parked in the spot Ruth and their houseboat recently vacated.

"Perfect," Eleanor nodded her approval. "I was hoping the police tape would still be in place. I'm ready to go to the office."

"You're in charge."

The women backtracked, making their way into the small and dreary space. A pungent odor filled the office. Margaret made a gagging sound.

"What is that awful smell?" Eleanor wheezed as she frantically waved her hand in front of her face.

"Catfish bait." The tall man behind the counter eyed Eleanor's blue housecoat with interest. "You two don't look like you're dressed for a day on the river."

"Looks can be deceiving." Eleanor quickly recovered as she inched toward the desk, a serious expression on her face. "My niece and I are hoping to rent a boat in the near future, the larger the better. It's for a family get-together. We're here to inquire on your rates and availability."

"I see." The man, *Fitz,* according to his nametag, reached for a three-ring binder. He flipped it open. "What date are you looking at?"

"It won't be for a couple of months...somewhere around mid-June." Eleanor threw a date out. "We haven't confirmed the reunion date."

"I have a twenty-four foot cruiser - a pontoon boat that seats thirteen. It rents for three hundred dollars a day and includes a full tank of gas."

"Three hundred bucks a day?" Margaret gasped.

"I think that's a fair price." Eleanor gave Margaret a sharp look. "My niece is the penny pincher of the family. Ignore her. I'm the one who'll be paying."

"I see. Would you like me to pencil you in?"

"Not yet. We took the liberty of walking along the pier, to check out the amenities and width of the marina since I have a little trouble backing up. I wanted to make sure the channel is wide enough."

Fitz lifted a brow. "Do you have a valid driver's license? You'll need a valid driver's license to rent one of my houseboats."

"Of course I do," Eleanor snapped.

"I meant no offense."

Margaret could see Eleanor, sensitive about her driving abilities, was getting a little hot under the housecoat. She attempted to shift the conversation. "We noticed there's police tape around one of the houseboats and wondered what happened."

"There was a minor incident earlier today. It's been taken care of," Fitz said.

"But there's police tape," Margaret answered. "Police tape is not used for 'minor incidents.'"

Fitz rubbed his brow and Margaret could see he was beginning to wish he'd never set eyes on them.

"A local, the owner of the houseboat, was found dead this morning."

"Oh dear." Eleanor's hand flew to her mouth. "Did the person drown?"

"Possibly," Fitz said vaguely. "The police are still investigating."

"That's terrible," Margaret said. "Did you know the person?"

"Unfortunately, yes," Fitz said. "Can I help you with anything else?"

Before the women answered, the office phone rang. "If you'll excuse me for a moment." Fitz lifted the receiver. "Sunshine Bridge Marina, Fitz Buchanan speaking."

Margaret wandered into the adjacent small store, one ear tuned in to what Fitz was saying. "Yes. The houseboat is still secure. I haven't checked on it for a couple of hours. I can't leave the office until one of my employees shows up at noon."

There was a pause as Fitz listened. "You say you're the lead investigator, Detective Flanders? I see. If you want to return to the marina, the employee who was on duty last night, Buddy Granger, will be here in about an hour. He told me this morning he thinks he might have some useful information."

Fitz told the investigator Buddy would be working at the marina until it closed at nine. He finished his conversation and hung up. "Can I help you with anything else?"

"No, I think that's all we need for now," Eleanor said. "Unless you have a brochure with your prices and a list of boats for rent."

"Of course." Fitz handed Eleanor a flyer and the women exited the office.

"Now what?" Margaret asked.

"Did you hear what Fitz said?" Eleanor motioned Margaret off to the side. "He was talking to the police about checking on Larry's houseboat."

"Right. He also mentioned he was working all alone for another hour or so, until Buddy someone showed up."

"Exactly. Which gives us enough time to sneak on board Larry's houseboat and have a look around."

Chapter 7

"This isn't going to work." Margaret shaded her eyes and scanned the marina. "There are too many people hanging around."

"You're right," Eleanor agreed. "We have an audience. They're already staring at us."

"It's your outfit. Not many people show up at a marina dressed in a housecoat."

"What's wrong with my outfit?" Eleanor patted her pocket. "Besides, judge not lest you be judged."

Margaret and Eleanor returned to the front of the parking lot and climbed into the van. "This mission was a bust."

"I thought I lost you," Ruth said.

"Eleanor came up with the bright idea to sneak on board Larry's houseboat to have a look around before we left."

"Way to go, Eleanor. Now you're sleuthing. What did you find?"

"We didn't. There were too many people hanging around and we were already drawing attention to ourselves." Margaret pointed at Eleanor.

"You don't like it when I dress in black. You don't like it when I dress like a little old lady. I can't win." Eleanor rolled her eyes and Ruth chuckled.

"I think your disguise is perfect." Ruth consulted the rearview mirror and shifted into reverse. "Besides, it would have been a waste of time. I'm sure the authorities went over Larry's houseboat with a fine tooth comb."

"While we were inside, Fitz, the owner, got a call from Detective Flanders. He plans to return to the marina and interview someone named Bud, the man who was working there last night."

"Buddy." Ruth thumped the steering wheel. "Now why didn't we think of that?"

"According to the owner, Buddy is starting his shift in about an hour and working until closing," Margaret said.

"I think it will be worth our time to talk to Buddy, but it will have to wait until later," Ruth said. "For now, we need to head back to the houseboat. Our surprise should be waiting for us."

*****

Liz Applegate tottered down the marina drive, one hand gripping the straw hat perched atop her head, her other holding onto a large piece of luggage. She hit a dip in the drive and tumbled forward.

The rut was no match for Liz, a pro in high heels, and she quickly recovered.

Several of the men working on their boats, stopped to check out the meticulously dressed woman, a real looker. Liz, in turn, rewarded them with a generous smile.

"Please tell me I'm seeing a mirage and not Liz," Gloria groaned. "I thought we were going to swing by her place for a cup of coffee and then leave."

"Isn't this much better? You haven't seen your sister in ages. Now you two can spend some time together catching up." Ruth traipsed to the end of the dock and began waving her arms.

Gloria reluctantly followed behind.

"Ruth, you look fabulous." Liz gave her two air kisses, one on each cheek before turning to her sister. "Hello, Gloria. I bet you're surprised to see me."

"Shocked is a better word. I thought we were stopping by your place for a cup of coffee while passing through."

"That was the original plan. When Ruth called and asked if I wanted to join you girls on your river adventure, I decided why not?"

Liz steered her luggage toward her sister. "Would you mind? These heels aren't conducive to lugging luggage and since you're wearing those ridiculously sensible flats, you'll have an easier time maneuvering it."

Gloria reached for the handle, mumbling softly under her breath. As much as she disliked the initial surprise of the houseboat adventure, it was nothing compared to being stuck on board the houseboat with her demanding sister, Liz, for the next couple of days.

A wave of sheer terror coursed through Gloria as a thought occurred to her. "You...you're not spending the *entire* week with us, are you?"

"Oh...I don't know," Liz said. "Ruth invited me. I haven't decided yet."

Gloria fleetingly wondered how mad Ruth and the others would be if she bailed on them and snuck off to the nearest resort.

Lucy, Dot, Margaret and the others gathered around, all talking at once and seemingly excited to see Liz. Gloria was the only one who was quiet as her sister rambled on about her fabulous Florida home, her boy toy boyfriend, Martin, and the lavish gifts he gave her.

She was tempted to mention the time Martin disappeared for weeks after Liz bought *him* a bunch of expensive items, but held her tongue. Gloria reminded herself she hadn't seen her sister in several months, not since the previous summer.

After catching up, Ruth gave Liz the grand tour of the houseboat and finished the tour on the open deck.

Liz cast a concerned look around. "Where am I going to sleep? I don't see an extra bed."

"There's a sleeper sofa in the living room," Ruth said. "The sleeper sofa is much larger than the bunks. You'll have plenty of room."

"Ruth, you are so thoughtful. I would much rather sleep in one of the bunks. Sleeper sofas hurt my back."

"I'll swap with you," Dot generously offered.

"How did you get here?" Gloria asked.

"Martin dropped me off. Ruth said she'd give me a ride home."

"Tomorrow?" Gloria asked hopefully.

"You're hilarious, Gloria." Liz punched her sister's arm playfully. "Always clowning around. I gather we're not staying in this...quaint little mom and pop marina. We need to find a place with more action, somewhere exciting."

"Oh, we have something exciting going on all right," Eleanor said.

"Now what did you do?" Liz pinned Gloria with a pointed stare.

"We found a body in a marina up the river," Ruth said.

98

"Maybe the person got a little tipsy, fell overboard and drowned."

"With his hands duct taped behind his back," Lucy said.

"I'm not surprised." Liz tsk-tsked. "We have some of the most unusual crimes here in Florida. You never know who you'll run into and what evil intentions they may have. Thank goodness we're not staying there."

"It's not that simple," Dot said. "Ruth kinda got into an argument with the dead guy yesterday at this marina. Somehow, his houseboat ended up next to ours at the other marina. Ruth and Gloria found him floating face down in the water this morning."

Liz turned to Ruth. "Did you take him out?"

"Of course I didn't." Ruth's face turned bright red. "He was a jerk, but I didn't kill him. I don't...didn't even know him."

"We can't leave until the investigators give us the okay," Rose said. "I knew I shoulda brought my special potion to ward off evil spirits. This houseboat is in definite need of some help. First, we crash into the side of the man's houseboat and then he's found dead, right next door."

"So we're stuck here at the marina for heaven knows how long?" Liz appeared genuinely horrified at the thought.

"No, we can leave the marina. We can't leave Florida," Margaret said. "Speaking of leaving, I think it's time to fly the coop."

"Let's pull anchor." Lucy motioned for Gloria to help her untie the houseboat. After untying both ends, they climbed on board and began drifting away from the dock.

Gloria noticed a long scrape along the side of the dock. She hollered up to Ruth, who was in the flybridge. "Hey, Ruth. Did you do that?"

"Do what?" Ruth leaned over the console.

"Scrape the side of the dock."

"Of course not. That's not funny." Ruth glared at Gloria as she gunned the motor.

Liz headed inside, complaining it was too hot. Gloria found an empty spot in the corner and eased onto the bench. She closed her eyes and tilted her head back, enjoying the warm sunshine.

They cruised the river for another hour before Ruth pulled the houseboat into a small cove and they all gathered on the open deck. "I don't know about you guys, but I'm starving. Dot's been hard at work, whipping up a breakfast feast."

"She has?" Gloria hadn't even noticed Dot wasn't with them. "I'll see if she needs help." She stepped inside and her mouth began to water at the tantalizing aroma of sizzling bacon.

Dot darted back and forth, from the stove to the sink, to the refrigerator, barely looking up.

"Dot Jenkins. You're supposed to be on vacation, not stuck in the kitchen making breakfast," Gloria scolded.

"You know I can't stay out of the kitchen. Besides, it keeps my mind off my worries."

"Let me help." Gloria dug through the drawers until she found a butter knife. "What kind of worries? If Liz is bothering you, I'll ask her to leave, or better yet toss her overboard. That would be fun."

"Liz is the least of my worries." Dot carefully placed the bacon on a layer of paper towels. "If anything, she'll liven the place up."

"Like we need more excitement. Then what's wrong?"

"It's about last night." Dot began chewing on her lower lip, a sign that she was troubled.

"What happened last night?"

"Earlier, one of the police officers questioned us about whether we heard or saw anything last night or this morning."

"Yes, and it was loud with the air conditioner running in our bunkhouse. We all agreed we didn't hear anything," Gloria said.

"I got to thinking about it, you know. I drank a lot of tea last night before I went to bed. I guess in all the excitement I drank a little too much. Anyways, I got up to use the bathroom and the small ceiling vent in the bathroom was open. While I was in there, I could've sworn I heard someone yelling."

"But you didn't mention it to the authorities."

"No. I was going to, but then I wasn't a hundred percent certain I heard it, after all."

"Do you remember what time?"

"It was the middle of the night." Dot shook her head. "I'm afraid to say anything now because they'll think I was withholding information."

"People remember stuff all of the time. Perhaps what you heard will help the authorities figure out the timeline of when Larry Molson went into the water. The lead investigator left us his card. After we finish breakfast, we can give him a call."

Dot nodded absentmindedly, a troubled look still firmly in place.

"There's something else."

"Yes."

"Something you're worried about," Gloria guessed.

Dot nodded again. She glanced out the slider at the others, who were chatting on the deck, everyone that is, except Eleanor, who swam by the kitchen window overlooking the cove.

"Eleanor is in the water." Gloria slid the kitchen window open and leaned out. "You do know there are alligators in the St. Johns River."

Eleanor stopped treading water and floated toward them. "They don't want me. I'm too old and tough to eat."

Gloria shook her head and closed the window.

"She's probably knocking off another item on her bucket list." Dot smiled. "I hope I have half her energy when I'm her age."

"Me too. Well?" Gloria asked.

"Well, what?"

"Something is seriously bothering you. It's written all over your face."

Dot briefly closed her eyes and sucked in a deep breath. "Right after I heard the hollering, I heard a muffled sound, like someone walking around. It was coming from the small deck up above, in the crow's nest where Ruth was sleeping."

"Maybe she heard it too," Gloria pointed out. "She got out of bed and went to check it out."

"But she never mentioned it to the investigators," Dot said. "Why wouldn't she mention it to the investigators?"

Chapter 8

"I don't know." Gloria mulled over Dot's confession as she buttered the toast. Why hadn't Ruth mentioned she heard someone holler...unless she hadn't heard anyone holler.

Surely, the air conditioner in the crow's nest was as noisy as the one in the bunkhouse. If so, then Ruth may not have heard anything, or maybe she heard something, but didn't realize it.

One thing was certain, Gloria and Ruth had been friends for decades. Unless her friend felt her life was in imminent danger she would not murder someone, not even someone as aggravating as Larry Molson.

When the food was ready, Gloria summoned everyone inside where they loaded their plates with hash browns, crispy slices of bacon, scrambled eggs and wheat toast.

"Gloria, why don't you pray," Dot said.

The women bowed their heads.

"Dear Heavenly Father. Thank you for this beautiful day. Thank you for bringing us together for this special time to make memories and enjoy each other's company. Thank you for allowing Liz to join us."

She continued. "Lord, you know our hearts are heavy over the death of Larry Molson. We pray you'll comfort his family and help the investigators figure out what happened to that poor man. Thank you for this food and most of all for your Son, our Savior, Jesus Christ. Amen."

"Amen," the women echoed.

Margaret bit the corner of her toast. "What's the plan for today, Ruth?"

"You mentioned visiting some springs nearby." Gloria scooped up a large spoonful of scrambled eggs.

"First on the list is a visit to the Blue Springs State Park." Ruth explained that the springs, one of the largest on the St. Johns River, were a designated manatee refuge. "During the winter and early spring months, the manatees migrate to the springs because they're warmer than the ocean."

Margaret cast a glance outdoors. "It's warm outside. Would the manatees still be hanging out in the springs?"

"I'm not sure, but I thought it was worth checking out."

"Will we see alligators?" Eleanor asked. "I'm still hoping to see at least one since I didn't spot any while I was swimming."

"Thank goodness," Dot said.

"I think gators prefer the river, not the springs," Ruth said. "After we visit the springs, there's another spot I want to check out, farther along the river."

Lucy reached for a slice of bacon. "How many nights will we be staying on the houseboat?"

"We have tonight and tomorrow night. I figured maybe later we could do a little fishing."

"I betcha there's some catfish here in the river. I used to love fishing for catfish," Rose said. "First, we're gonna need some fish food."

"Buddy," Ruth and Gloria said in unison. "Buddy sells catfish bait."

"I see a plan shaping up," Margaret said. "It would be the perfect excuse to return to the Sunshine Bridge Marina and question Buddy about Larry Molson."

"Who is Buddy?" Liz asked.

"He's the guy we met when we registered for last night's stay at the Sunshine Bridge Marina. He's a real character," her sister explained. "His homemade catfish bait smells gross."

"The smellier, the better," Rose said. "Can we stop back by there and pick some up before we go fishing?"

"Of course," Ruth said.

"I'm not sure how good I'm gonna be at interrogating," Rose said. "Can't someone else do it?"

"Buddy already met Ruth and me," Gloria said. "Lucy was with us when the police showed up. Margaret and Eleanor were there earlier, which leaves you and Dot."

"I guess we're up," Dot said. "We're team players, right Rose?"

"I...suppose. Heaven help me. I have no idea how I get involved in such shenanigans."

Gloria smiled. "You'll be fine. Ruth also had a great idea. She mentioned dropping by the Gator House Restaurant to talk to Darcy, the waitress."

Ruth stood. "I called the restaurant while you were making breakfast. Darcy isn't working until later this afternoon. We'll visit the springs, then start cruising back toward Gator House Landing, the marina where we rented the houseboat and the scene of our first run in with Molson."

Gloria followed Ruth into the kitchen. "Hopefully, the police are on their way to the restaurant now and will be long gone by the time we get there."

"I don't think that should stop us." Lucy polished off the last of her hash browns. "After all, we rented the houseboat from Gator House and the restaurant is a public place. We have a legitimate reason to be there."

"I agree, but it will be hard to question Darcy if the authorities are there."

The women made quick work of cleaning up the breakfast dishes while Ruth settled in behind the controls and they coasted out of the cove.

The women took turns getting ready in the bathroom, slipping into their swimsuits and slathering on a thick layer of sunscreen.

Dot and Rose carried one of the Styrofoam coolers onto the deck and passed out bottled waters.

Gloria found a sunny spot near the front while Liz huddled under the awning. "Aren't you going to get some sun?"

"No way." Liz shook her head. "It brings out my freckles and Martin doesn't like freckles. He thinks they're ugly."

"Who..." Gloria started to say, "Who cares what Martin likes?" She wisely decided to keep her comment to herself. Although she'd never met Martin, the stunts he'd pulled on her sister left a bitter taste in her mouth.

Instead, she decided to discuss a safer subject. "How is Frances?" Frances, Liz's best friend, had moved to Florida with Liz. They both lived in the same housing community.

"She's lost her ever-loving mind."

"Why do you say that?"

"She moved in with her boyfriend, Harvey. He's got some big bucks." Liz rubbed her fingers together. "He has poor Frances jumping through hoops. He treats her like his maid, his chauffeur, his cook. Frances swears she and Harvey are madly in love, but I've got his number." Liz made a small 'hmpf' noise and leaned her head back.

Lucy, who was sitting nearby listening in, lifted her head. "His number?"

"He's a womanizer with a wandering eye. He even hit on me once."

"Did you mention it to Frances?" Gloria asked.

"Yes. She accused me of making it up because I was jealous and wished I was dating someone rich like Harvey instead of a gigolo boyfriend. That was a couple of months ago. Now, whenever we pass each other in our golf carts, Frances won't even look at me."

"I'm sorry to hear that." Gloria genuinely liked Frances. She remembered the time Frances and Liz still lived in Michigan and she was obsessed with Milton Tilton. He'd gone missing from the retirement community where the three of them lived. Gloria and her friends helped by figuring out what had happened to him.

"He'll show his true colors soon enough," Lucy predicted. "If he's a player for real, she'll catch on. Frances isn't stupid."

"You wouldn't know it by how she's acting," Liz muttered.

"Lucy is right. If Harvey is a womanizer, Frances will eventually find out on her own. You're a good friend to Frances and I know you'll be there for her if...or when he breaks her heart."

"It's getting hot out here." Liz slid off the seat. "I think I'll head inside and keep Ruth company."

Gloria waited until her sister disappeared inside the houseboat. "I still don't get a good feeling about Liz's boyfriend, Martin."

"Maybe you should ask Liz if we can meet him when we drop her off," Lucy suggested.

"What a great idea. I think I will." Gloria closed her eyes and leaned her head back. The gentle motion of the houseboat almost put her to sleep. The day was turning into a scorcher. She could feel her face overheating, so she took over Liz's empty spot in the shade and watched the others.

Ruth steered the houseboat toward a docking area. When they got close, Lucy stepped onto the shore and tied up next to a smaller boat.

"Where are we?" Rose asked.

"We're near the entrance to the Blue Springs State Park. We'll have to hoof it from here."

"I've already visited the springs." Liz waved dismissively. "I'll stay here and keep an eye on the houseboat."

"Are you sure?" Ruth asked.

"Positive."

The others joined Lucy and began walking along a dirt path leading through some thick scrub brush.

Gloria swatted at several spider webs and jumped every time she heard rustling in the bushes, certain that Eleanor's alligator sighting was around every corner.

Finally, they reached a clearing and a paved sidewalk with signs leading to the springs.

Sweat poured off Gloria's brow and her damp clothes clung to her. The thought of diving into the springs and cooling off grew more appealing by the minute.

They made a brief stop at the park ranger station where they discovered the manatees had already left the springs.

"Can we swim in the springs?" Lucy fanned her face. It was turning the same shade of red as her hair.

"Yes, the springs are open for swimming."

The women thanked the man and trudged the rest of the way along the gravel drive, through the parking lot and finally, to the springs.

The sound of laughter echoed through the trees and Gloria could hear people splashing in the water. "We're close."

"I see them." Eleanor ran ahead and was the first to dive into the crystal clear waters. Ruth jumped in next, followed by Lucy. Dot and Margaret slowly descended the side ladder while Rose insisted all she wanted to do was dip her toes in the water.

Gloria was the last one in. It took a minute to adjust to the chilly water. Soon, she was swimming around, enchanted by how clear the water was and how far down she could see.

After swimming, they meandered along the wooden walkways to the overlook for a view of the deepest part and the springhead.

The friends retraced their steps and then stopped by the gift shop for ice cream and souvenirs. After purchasing their sweet treats, they sat under a shade tree to enjoy them.

"Thanks for bringing us to the springs," Dot said. "They're beautiful."

"And refreshing," Lucy said. "I'm definitely not used to this hot sun."

"You're welcome." Ruth polished off the last of her cone. "Now that we've eaten our dessert, we'll head back to the houseboat to make lunch."

The women tossed the wrappers in the trash and began the trek back. When they got there, they found Liz napping on the living room sofa.

Her eyes flew open when Ruth opened the slider door. "You're back already?"

"We've been gone for a couple of hours," Gloria said.

The women changed their clothes and then joined Ruth, who was barbecuing on one of the park's grills.

"Something smells delicious." Gloria sniffed appreciatively. "All of this fresh air and exercise is making me hungry."

"Me too." Margaret peeked over Ruth's shoulder at the grilling hotdogs.

Ruth playfully snapped the tongs in Margaret's direction. "No sneaking samples."

"I wouldn't dream of it. It's my turn to help in the kitchen. I'll go fix the corn on the cob."

"Are you going to grill it? There isn't enough room, plus it will take too long." Dot followed Margaret inside.

"Isn't it your turn to take a break?"

"You know I can't stay out of the kitchen."

"I was thinking of boiling the corn."

"There's a better way." Dot reached into one of the overhead cabinets and pulled out a box of plastic wrap. "The corn is in the fridge. I already husked it."

Margaret grabbed the corn from the refrigerator and set it on the counter. She watched as Dot removed a few loose strands of husk and then wrapped four pieces in plastic wrap, making sure to cover the ends.

She repeated the process with the remaining pieces before placing them in the microwave and turning it on.

"I've never microwaved corn on the cob," Margaret said.

"The plastic acts like a steamer. You don't lose all of the nutrients like you do when you boil it in water."

"Ah." Margaret lifted a brow. "I guess you're never too old to learn something new."

While the corn cooked, the women gathered the condiments for the hotdogs and arranged them in assembly line fashion.

The rest of the women followed Ruth and the large platter of hotdogs inside, each complimenting Ruth on her master grilling techniques and Dot for making the perfectly cooked corn on the cob.

While they ate, Liz told them about a bird sanctuary she'd heard about, not far from where they were docked.

"I'm surprised we haven't heard from the detective investigating Larry's death." Gloria swallowed her last sip of soda and wiped her mouth.

"He may have." Ruth patted her pockets. "Shoot. I stuck it in my backpack before we hiked over to the springs." She sprang from her seat and hurried to her backpack, propped up in the corner.

She unzipped the front, reached inside and pulled out her phone. "I have one missed call." Ruth punched in her four-digit code. Her eyes widened as she listened to the message. "I can't believe it. You've got to hear this."

Chapter 9

Ruth hit the speaker button on her cell phone and held it up. "This is Detective Flanders of the Volusia County Sheriff's Department. It appears Mr. Molson filed a complaint against you for destroying personal property and for harassment. I would like to arrange a meeting."

The detective finished by asking Ruth to call him back as soon as possible. He rattled off his cell phone number and the call ended.

"Good grief." Ruth tossed her cell phone on the counter. "I barely nicked his stinkin' houseboat and I certainly wasn't harassing him."

"Hopefully, Darcy, the waitress, will be able to shed a little more light on Molson's background. Maybe he was in the habit of filing complaints," Gloria said.

Ruth returned the call and left a message for Detective Flanders. "I guess I'll have to wait for him to call back."

"Why don't we head back to the Gator House Restaurant to talk to Darcy," Gloria suggested. "By the time we get there, she should be starting her shift."

"Might as well," Ruth said glumly. "Not that it will help."

"You don't know that," Gloria chided. "So Molson filed a complaint. It doesn't make you a killer."

When they reached the Gator House Landing and the restaurant, Ruth steered the houseboat into an empty spot. She shut the engine off while Lucy secured the boat. Gloria joined her on the dock.

"Ruth is upset," Lucy said. "I don't blame her."

"Me either. I'm hoping the waitress will be able to help us figure out who was with Molson on the dock the other day."

Ruth and the others joined Lucy and Gloria. "I don't hold out much hope for this. I'm a goner."

"You're not a goner and you're not a quitter," Gloria said.

The women headed inside the Gator House Restaurant where Darcy, the server, had just arrived. She immediately recognized the women and darted to the entryway. "You're back?"

"Yes. We were hoping we might be able to chat with you for a minute. It's about Larry Molson," Gloria explained.

"He's dead," Darcy said. "I heard he was found floating face down in the Sunshine Bridge Marina this morning."

"Yes, and we found him," Ruth said.

Darcy's eyes grew wide. "Oh my gosh. You're kidding."

"I wish we were," Gloria said. "It appears Mr. Molson was upset with us and filed a complaint against Ruth with the county sheriff's office."

"Because you bumped his boat."

"You heard?" Margaret asked.

"Yes. He was furious after it happened. He hadn't had much luck with his houseboat lately. Larry stormed back in here looking for more witnesses because he planned to report it to the authorities."

"There were two men on the dock with Mr. Molson at the time Ruth nicked his boat."

A man approached the group and nudged Darcy. "You have some customers waiting for their food. It's up."

"I'm on my way, Roy."

Gloria watched the man return to the bar. "Is that your boss?"

"Yes. He's the owner, Mr. Paver. We're short-staffed today. I need to get back to work."

126

"We'll sit at one of your tables," Dot blurted out. "Which section is yours?"

Darcy pointed to her area and the women strolled over to the barstools. Gloria climbed up on one and reached for a menu. "We should at least order something."

They were still studying the menus when Darcy hurried over. "We make some delicious frozen drinks."

"I'm in the mood for a fruity concoction," Liz said. "I'll take the Bahama mama."

"What's in it?" Lucy's eyes squinted as she studied the menu.

"Strawberries, pineapple, white chocolate and coconut," Darcy rattled off. "The berry bliss is delish. It's made with blueberries, strawberries, raspberries and blackberries and one of my favorites."

"I like berries." Gloria tucked the menu in the holder. "I'll have that."

127

Darcy finished taking their orders and made her way to the ticket counter. They waited for her to return with their drinks before Ruth spoke. "Did Larry find anyone to corroborate his claim of me damaging his houseboat?"

"Nope." Darcy shook her head. "Larry had a reputation around here and it wasn't a good one. Most people who knew him didn't like him."

Gloria had a hunch she knew why, but figured it wouldn't hurt to ask. "What kind of reputation?"

"Larry was a troublemaker. He was always looking for someone to sue." Darcy glanced around and lowered her voice. "Mr. Paver, the owner of the restaurant, nicknamed him Lawsuit Larry. He sued the county claiming the county boat ramp damaged his truck. I think he even filed suits against some of the other marinas."

Gloria's mind whirled as Darcy made her way to a nearby table. If what she said was true, Larry had his share of enemies, perhaps even someone at the other marina where they found his body.

A disturbing thought popped into Gloria's head. "What if someone set Ruth up to take the fall?" It would be the perfect opportunity to take troublemaker Larry out and make it look like Ruth, who was involved in a very public run in with Larry, murdered him.

"The doo doo is getting deeper by the minute." Lucy sipped her smoothie. "It could be someone witnessed Ruth's minor mishap and Larry's harsh words. The killer followed us to the other marina and then at some point during the night, murdered him."

"How convenient that his houseboat was parked right next to ours," Eleanor pointed out.

Gloria drummed her fingers on the tabletop. "It does seem like an unusual coincidence. Ruth argued with Larry. She scraped his houseboat. He ends up next to us in the marina and his body is floating in between our houseboats early the next morning. It could be Larry's killer drove the boat to the marina after murdering him and then tossed his body over the side."

"We need to find out who Larry was with at the time of our altercation," Ruth said.

Darcy returned to check on them and Lucy posed the question. "Yesterday, when we were here, Larry was with two other men. We were wondering who they might be."

"I...don't recall noticing who Larry was with."

"Too bad we don't have a picture of them," Gloria said.

"Hang on." Eleanor flashed her cell phone. "Remember yesterday when I was taking pictures before we left?" She turned her attention to the phone. "Will you look at that? I have a picture of Larry and the other men are in the background."

Gloria took the phone from her friend. She zoomed in on the picture and then handed it to Darcy. "Do you recognize these men?"

"Yep. One of them is Larry's brother, Ike. I'm surprised they're together."

"Why is that?" Ruth asked.

"Because Larry decked his brother a couple of weeks ago when they got into a brawl on the dock." Darcy blew air through thinned lips. "It got ugly. Roy ended up calling the cops when Ike pulled a gun."

"Oh my." Eleanor pressed a hand to her chest. "I've never seen a shootout before, only on television."

"Please don't add it to your bucket list," Lucy said.

"A lot of strange things happen here in Florida. I think I'll pass on that one," Eleanor said. "Do you have any idea why they were fighting?"

Darcy shrugged. "It's hard telling with Larry and Ike. They're...colorful characters. Ike is about as popular around here as Larry was." She tapped the screen to enlarge the picture. "That's what I thought."

"Thought what?" Gloria asked.

"The other man, standing on the dock with Larry and his brother, Ike, is Soaring Eagle."

"Soaring Eagle?" Ruth leaned over Darcy's shoulder.

"He's the caretaker at Crimson Hall."

Gloria perked up. "What is Crimson Hall?"

"It's a historic plantation/estate about half a mile up the river. The county owns it and it's haunted as all get out." Darcy shivered. "Soaring Eagle is a Native American, I think from the Seminole Tribe. He lives in the caretaker's cottage behind Crimson Hall."

"Why would he be with Larry Molson?" Lucy interrupted.

"Soaring Eagle is the self-appointed river patrol. He probably caught Larry speeding in a no-wake zone, or some other small offense and Soaring Eagle followed him here to warn him to knock it off. He knows everything that happens on the river. I would watch out for him."

Ruth stirred her smoothie and took a sip. "You said Crimson Hall is not far from here?"

"Yep." Darcy explained the estate offered daily guided tours of both the home and the grounds. "They close at six. You should go early if you're going to visit. They have a docking area on the river. You can park the houseboat while you take the tour."

"It sounds fascinating," Eleanor gushed. "A haunted house."

"It sounds creepy and a place to avoid at all costs," Liz said.

"I want to check it out," Margaret said. "I bet they have some fantastic antiques on display."

A couple at the table behind them motioned to get Darcy's attention. "I better get back to work."

Gloria waited until Darcy left. "The list of suspects is growing."

"I think it was either Ike, the brother, or Soaring Eagle, who took Molson out," Margaret said. "They were with Molson only hours before his death."

While the others chatted, Ruth fiddled with her cell phone. After they left, she lagged behind. Gloria let the others go ahead as she waited for Ruth. "Are you all right? You seem distracted."

"I have a lot on my mind. Whether Detective Flanders is saying it or not, I'm a prime suspect in Molson's murder." Ruth slowed even more. "While you were talking, I decided to do a little search on the internet for Larry Molson."

"Did you find anything?"

"Yep. He owns Molson & Molson Detective Agency in Orlando."

"Seriously?" Gloria abruptly stopped. "Molson was a PI?"

"It appears so. I didn't have time to delve deeper. He made a few headlines lately, and I caught a glimpse of an article about his recent lawsuits. I was going to wait until I could find a quiet spot to do a little more research."

Back at the houseboat, the women gathered in the living room area while Ruth briefly explained what she'd found.

"Maybe Molson stepped on a few toes during his investigations and someone took a contract out on him," Eleanor theorized.

"You watch too many crime thrillers," Dot teased.

"It could be true," Eleanor insisted.

"His detective agency is Molson & Molson...I wonder who the other Molson is," Gloria said.

"His brother?" Lucy guessed.

"Could be."

"I'm going to run up to the crow's nest and call Detective Flanders again. Maybe this time he'll answer. I want to let him know what we found. After that, I'm going to do a little more digging around on my laptop before we leave. The cell signal on the river is non-existent, so I want to log onto the internet while we're here."

"I'll go with you." Gloria followed her friend up the spiral staircase.

Ruth tried the detective's cell phone first and left another message. "I hope he calls me back before we leave here. Let's see what else we can find out about Molson."

The women discovered Larry Molson and his brother, Ike, were partners at the detective agency. The previous year, Molson & Molson exposed a high profile attorney who was having an affair with a local district attorney.

The story made headlines and there were several interviews with Larry and his brother, Ike. "Maybe the attorney who got busted took him out," Gloria said.

"Or the district attorney." Ruth clicked on another news story. The information was almost identical to the previous story. "We're going in circles now. There's no new information."

"You're right." Gloria popped off the stool and began pacing. "My gut tells me there are more clues over at the Sunshine Bridge Marina. We need to get Rose in there to try to find out what Buddy, the man who was working last night, knows."

Chapter 10

"What if he doesn't believe me?" Rose clasped her hands. "I ain't never spearheaded one of your investigations before. What if I screw it up?"

Eleanor squeezed Rose's arm. "If I can do it, so can you. Besides, you're there for a legitimate reason. You're looking for catfish bait."

"And I'll be with you," Dot said. "We'll ask a few simple questions, grab the bait and leave."

"I am looking forward to trying my hand at fishing and if the stinky fish bait is halfway decent, we'll be eating grilled catfish for dinner." Cheered by the thought of fishing, Rose followed Dot to the marina store.

The bell clanged loudly as the women stepped inside. Dot curled her lip at the unpleasant odor. "Yuck."

"That's my catfish bait." The man rapped his knuckles on the counter. "It's an acquired smell. The fish love it. How can I help you lovely ladies?"

"As a matter of fact, I'm in the market for catfish bait," Rose said. "A friend of mine said you carry a special brand."

"That I do." He eyed Rose curiously. "You ever been catfishing before?"

"A long time ago. I'm always open to pointers Mr...."

"Buddy Granger. My friends call me Buddy."

"And my name is Rose Morris," Rose said. "I'm all ears."

"Well, the most important thing is the bait." Buddy reached behind him and grabbed a jar. "This here is the best catfish bait money can buy."

"Is this the stuff that stinks?" Dot asked.

"It is, and the smellier the better. If you use my catfish bait, I *guarantee* you'll catch some catfish."

"You guarantee it?" Rose asked.

"Yep." Buddy nodded. "Or your money back."

"It's tempting and sounds like an offer I can't refuse." Rose reached for her purse.

"Don't you want to hear my other tips?"

"Of course."

"You gotta fish with the barb of your hook exposed. Don't go covering it up. I'll show you what I mean." Buddy picked up a fishing pole and carried it to the counter where he proceeded to show Rose how to set her hook and add the stink bait.

The two became involved in a lengthy discussion about fishing. Dot, bored with the conversation, wandered out of the office and into the adjacent store. She inspected a small display of hunting and fishing magazines before perusing the candy aisle.

Dot grabbed a pack of Hershey's assorted chocolates and returned to the counter. "I heard one of the locals was found floating in your marina this morning."

Buddy's head shot up. "Yeah. It was an unfortunate incident. The authorities aren't talking yet."

"I heard the man, some sort of private investigator, wasn't too popular around here."

"You heard the truth. Larry was always sticking his nose in where it didn't belong and he was sue happy. Got him the nickname of Lawsuit Larry. Rumor 'round here is that he had a few of the local officials in his pocket."

"Really?" Dot lifted a brow. "You think he paid them off?"

"Knowing Larry, he wouldn't be above greasing a few palms to make a quick buck."

"I thought private investigators were held to a higher standard," Dot said. "If he was involved in shady dealings, the authorities could strip him of his license." She had a sudden thought. "Are private investigators licensed in Florida?"

"Yes, ma'am, at least I think so." Buddy leaned back, giving Dot his full attention. "You seem mighty curious about Mr. Molson. Did you know him?"

"No. I...I'm visiting the area." Dot smiled weakly. "Just making conversation."

"Huh." Buddy studied her for a second longer and then resumed his conversation with Rose.

Dot set the candy on the counter and noticed an open three-ring binder nearby. She leaned forward in an attempt to read the words. "I'm sure you stay busy this time of year."

"We do. Back in the day, we would take overnights on a first-come, first-serve basis, but now it's by reservation only, especially during peak season." Buddy propped the fishing pole against the counter. "What kind of fishing pole do you have, Rose?"

"I don't know. What kind should I use?"

"You gotta have a good one; otherwise, one good catfish'll come along and snap your pole, especially if you're using my special catfish bait. They love the stuff."

Rose looked disappointed. "I hope we have good poles."

"I like you Rose Morris and I can see you're going to make an excellent fisherwoman." Buddy picked the pole back up. "Tell you what, I'm gonna let you borrow one of my favorite fishing poles, if you promise to bring it back and tell me how many big ole catfish you caught with the tips I gave you and using the best catfish bait in Florida."

"Really? Are you sure, Buddy?" Rose's eyes lit as he presented her with the fishing pole.

"I insist. Let me show you a couple of quick tips. This pole is a little tricky." Buddy shot Dot a quick glance. "We're gonna step outside to cast the line real quick."

"I'll wait in here," Dot smiled.

"We'll be right back." Buddy followed Rose outside, leaving the office door open.

Dot waited until they were out of sight before snatching the binder off the counter. The top sheet listed the current day's reservations. She flipped the top sheet and scanned the sheet underneath...the previous day's reservations.

She easily found Ruth's name, along with a list of other names. She didn't see a reservation for Larry Molson.

Thud. Dot cast a quick glance over her shoulder at the sound of Rose's laughter and a dull thud.

When Buddy and Rose didn't appear, she hurriedly scanned the list a second time to confirm her suspicions that Larry Molson's name was not on the reservation list.

Dot slid the open binder across the counter moments before Buddy and Rose made their way back inside.

"Buddy, I sure do appreciate all of your help," Rose said. "If I catch me a mess of catfish, I'm gonna save the biggest one for you."

"That's mighty kind of you, Rose. I got one last word of warning. Watch out for Soaring Eagle. He's the self-appointed river patrol and spends most of his time cruising up and down the river. He's a good friend of mine. If you've never met him, he'll scare the dickens out of you."

"We heard about Soaring Eagle over at the Gator House Restaurant. He lives somewhere around here and works as a caretaker," Rose said.

"Yep. He works at Crimson Hall. If you have a hankerin' for history and ghosts, you'll want to stop by and check it out. They close early, before dark." Buddy leaned his elbows on the counter. "Most locals avoid the area after sunset. If you're gonna go fishing, steer clear of Crimson Bay."

Dot swallowed hard, as visions of ghastly ghosts filled her head. "How will we know if we're in Crimson Bay?"

"You can't miss it. The bay is nice enough. When you get closer to the shore, there's a small cemetery atop the hill. It's where Edward T. Parker, the wealthy river merchant who built Crimson Hall, is buried."

"The Parker family is buried in the plot?" Rose shifted the pole to her other hand.

"Nope. The Indians scared the Parker family off after they raided the hall, demanding their land back."

"Did the Indians scalp Mr. Parker?"

"Of course not," Buddy snorted. "Although death by scalping would make a much more exciting story. He holed up in the house after the Indians surrounded his home and refused to leave. His family was hiding in the back the entire time. The police showed up to try to diffuse the situation, Parker mistook them for Indians trying to break in and started shooting."

"What happened?" Dot asked.

"The police returned fire and killed Parker."

"Did the Indians end up getting the property after the family left the area?" Rose tightened her grip on the pole.

"Nope. Crimson Hall sat vacant for many years. It was vandalized by teens and thieves stripped the place of all of its valuables. Some famous actress purchased it with plans to fix it up. Months turned into years and nothing happened. Finally, the local historical society purchased it. They began restoring it about a decade ago."

"I guess Parker is the one haunting the place," Rose said.

"If I had to put money on it, I reckon so." Buddy rapped his knuckles on the counter. "You should check it out for yourselves. Crimson Hall will give you a good idea of what old Florida looked like, back before the big mouse, along with castles and amusement park rides moved in and Central Florida became all commercialized."

147

"Thank you for the tip," Dot said. "In the meantime, we better get going if Rose wants to try her hand at fishing tonight."

Rose waited for Dot to pay for the candy before handing Buddy the money for the stink bait. "I'll bring the pole back in the morning. That and the catfish I plan to catch."

"Let me give you my cell phone number, Rose. That way, if you got any questions, you can give me a call."

Buddy and Rose exchanged cell phone numbers, and the women exited the store. "That went better than I thought it would," Rose said.

"You did great," Dot said.

"But I didn't ask Buddy any questions."

"I think I covered what we needed to find out plus some bonus clues," Dot said. "Buddy took a real shine to you."

"We were talking fishing. He gave me some good fishing tips."

The women made their way back to the houseboat parked at the far end, near the fueling pumps and the snack shack.

Ruth waved a half-eaten ice cream cone. "You bought a fishing pole and stink bait?"

"I borrowed it." Rose propped the pole in the corner. "Where did you get the ice cream?"

"From the snack shack." Lucy licked the side of her cookies and cream cone. "We couldn't resist."

"We ate ice cream earlier at the springs," Dot pointed out.

"So?" Ruth bit the edge of her waffle cone. "We're on vacation and we can eat ice cream all day if we want."

"Liz isn't eating ice cream," Dot said.

"I'm trying to watch my girlish figure." Liz patted her hips. "Besides, Martin doesn't like chunky women."

"Martin schmartin," Gloria mumbled.

"Are you calling us fat?" Margaret joked.

"No." Liz frowned. "Of course not. I'm talking about me."

"I think I'll have some, too." Dot studied the list of ice creams and decided on a single scoop of toasted coconut in a small cup.

"Well?" Gloria waited until Dot joined them. "I see Rose picked up some stink bait."

"I found out something very interesting." Dot told them what Buddy said.

"This confirms our suspicions," Ruth said. "Any number of people could've taken Molson out."

"There's one more thing." Dot scooped a small spoonful of ice cream into her mouth. "Larry Molson didn't have a reservation last night."

Gloria paused, her spoon midair. "Are you sure?"

"Positive."

While they finished eating, Gloria pondered the clue. The Sunshine Bridge Marina rented slips by reservation only, yet Molson didn't have a reservation. Had he pulled in, hoping to snag a spot? Had he parked his houseboat in someone else's spot? "Dot, were the reservations numbered?"

"What do you mean by numbered?"

"The reservation binder...did you notice if there were assigned slips?"

"I can answer that," Ruth said. "When I called to make the reservation, the person on the phone gave me a slip number. I knew which slip to pull into when we got here."

"So...whose slip was Larry Molson parked in?" Gloria asked.

"I don't know. It's something we need to find out," Ruth said.

Rose pointed to the fishing pole Buddy had loaned her. "I promised to return Buddy's fishing pole tomorrow morning. Maybe we can have another look around the office."

"I want to check the slip number that was next to ours." While the others finished their ice cream, Gloria strolled to the end of the dock, noting the slip number where Larry's houseboat was parked.

She waved to the man at the snack shack and then joined her friends. "We need to ask the employee at the snack shack if he saw or heard anything."

"I already did. He was off yesterday and just got here to start his shift today," Ruth said. "Did you buy enough stink bait?"

"I hope so. I also got some excellent tips on catfishing. Buddy recommended trying the same cove we visited earlier, where Eleanor went swimming."

"Well, what are we waiting for?" Ruth said. "We need to go catch our dinner."

When they reached the fishing spot, Dot, Rose, Gloria and Lucy each cast a line while Liz, Margaret, Ruth and Eleanor watched.

Gloria glanced at Eleanor, sitting nearby. "Is fishing on your bucket list?"

"No way." Eleanor waved a hand. "I did plenty of fishing when Matthew was alive. I'll pass, thank you very much, but if you see an alligator...oh, that reminds me." Eleanor ran inside. She returned, carrying a pair of binoculars. "If there's a gator out there, I'll find it."

"I never thought to bring binoculars."

"These are special binoculars." Eleanor handed them to Gloria. "They have a special night vision coating on them. The darker it gets, the better they work."

"I see." Gloria handed them back. "I hope they help you spot the biggest gator out there, at a safe distance, of course."

The women spent a good hour fishing, trying a variety of different lures. Rose stuck to the stink bait Buddy sold her. Gloria wasn't sure if it was the bait, the pole or Buddy's tips, but Rose's techniques filled a bucket with fish.

"I think we have enough fish to clean and cook." Ruth held up the bucket.

"Hang on." Rose took a step back and tugged on her line. "I think I got me the granddaddy of all catfish."

"The fishing pole is bending." Gloria leaned forward to help Rose hold the pole. "I don't think the pole is strong enough."

"I can't let the big one get away," Rose grunted as she gave the pole a sharp jerk, right before they heard a loud *snap*.

Chapter 11

"What was that?" Lucy dropped her fishing pole and hustled to the other side of the boat.

"I broke the pole," Rose gasped. "I mean, I broke Buddy's pole. How was I to know it was going to snap in half?"

"And the big one got away." Gloria peered into the murky water.

"The big one getting away is the least of my worries." Rose rubbed her finger over the jagged end of the pole. "I'm going to have to buy Buddy a new pole. How can I replace it with another pole? It was one of his favorites."

"The end is stuck on the front railing." Gloria wiggled it loose and held it up for closer inspection. "It snapped clean off. We can try to tape it back together."

"Tape it back together?" Rose took the piece from Gloria. "With what?"

"There's some tape in the box of goodies the marina gave us," Ruth said. "I saw it when I was looking for a lighter to light the grill."

"I'll start cleaning the fish while you repair the pole and fire up the grill." Lucy grabbed the bucket of fish and carried it to shore.

Gloria fumbled around in the tackle box Buddy had also loaned Rose and held up a roll of duct tape. "Duct tape, the answer for everything."

"Except fixing someone's favorite fishing pole," Rose said glumly. "I knew I shouldn't have borrowed it."

"It's not your fault." Gloria ripped off a chunk of tape and began wrapping it around the pieces of pole. "It's the fish's fault. Butter Buddy up - tell him his pole almost got the big one."

Rose sighed heavily. "The stink bait sure did work like a charm. I not only caught catfish, but some bass, too."

"We have plenty of fish for dinner." Lucy finished cleaning the fish while Ruth dumped charcoal into the grill.

"I have a special recipe for grilled fish I've been itching to try. I found it online. We'll have to let the fish marinate for a little while. It will give the charcoal time to get going." Ruth carried the tray of filleted fish inside.

While they waited, the women chatted about home, wondering how Johnnie and Ray were managing Dot's Restaurant while Dot and Rose were gone.

Gloria suspected Paul was enjoying a couple of days on his own, fishing on the lake and spending time with his children. She popped off the bench seat. "I'm going to give Paul a call to check in."

She grabbed her cell phone and headed to a quiet spot on the shore. Gloria's call went directly to voice mail. She left a brief message, telling him they were on a houseboat and having a good time.

Gloria didn't mention Larry Molson's death or Liz joining them. Before disconnecting the line, she told him she loved him and if he tried to call back, he might not get through because of the poor cell reception.

She shoved the phone in her pocket and wandered back on board the boat.

"Well?" Ruth asked. "How are things back home?"

"Paul didn't answer. I left a voice mail."

"I called Kenny at the post office, while we were waiting for Dot and Rose to question Buddy."

"How is Kenny doing?" Gloria asked.

"He's cranky as all get-out. A postal employee from one of the other post offices is covering for me.

158

Kenny said she's a blabbermouth, talking non-stop. Poor guy."

Ruth glanced at her watch. "The recipe calls for marinating the fish a while longer, but it's getting late and I want to head out of here before dark." She ran inside and returned with the tray of fish. "I hope this is half as good as the reviews claim it is."

Soon the tantalizing aroma of grilled fish filled the air.

Dot eyed the fish thoughtfully. "Fish and chips sound good."

"I say we stick with something easy for a side dish," Gloria said. "I thought I saw some potato salad and coleslaw in the fridge."

"You did. I'll start setting everything up." Dot headed inside while Ruth and Lucy stacked the grilled fish on a clean plate and carried it to the kitchen.

The women arranged an assembly line of food, filling their plates with the grilled fish, along with the sides. Dot had also picked up dinner rolls and they feasted on the food as they discussed Larry's death.

Ruth tore off a chunk of her dinner roll. "I say we return Buddy's broken pole in the morning, and then head over to Crimson Hall to check it out."

"I'm not going inside," Rose said stubbornly. "Not if the place is haunted."

"You can hang out with Liz." Gloria turned to Ruth. "I was thinking about...Larry, aka Lawsuit Larry's death. We have two suspects; Larry's brother and Soaring Eagle. What about other lawsuits? The potential defendants would also be suspect."

"Darcy claims everybody knows everybody's business here on the river," Ruth said. "Surely, someone would know."

"Don't forget Larry didn't have a reservation at the Sunshine Bridge Marina. Buddy made a point of telling us reservations were required," Dot said.

"Perhaps the marina wasn't sold out and Larry took it upon himself to sneak into an empty spot and stay for free," Lucy theorized.

"Which happened to be right beside us," Ruth said. "I suppose if Larry was a local, he knew the marina office closed at nine. He could've easily pulled in after Buddy left for the day."

"Something isn't adding up." Gloria sawed off a piece of fish. "This fish is delicious, Ruth. What's in the marinade?"

"The recipe is fairly simple. It includes olive oil, lemon juice, garlic and soy sauce. You like it?"

"It's delicious," Lucy said.

The others unanimously agreed Rose's fish and Ruth's seasoning were a big hit.

"Back to Larry's death," Gloria said. "It could be Larry's brother, Ike, was with him on the houseboat the night of his death, which would make him the number one suspect."

"It would help if we knew who was with Larry or if he was alone." Gloria glanced around. "Do any of you remember seeing another houseboat before we went to bed?"

"I don't recall. I did take a few pictures of the houseboat and marina with my cell phone before we turned in last night," Lucy said. "I think Eleanor was taking pictures, too."

"You're right. She thought she saw a gator," Gloria said.

"To be honest, I forgot all about them until now. We haven't stopped to take a breather since finding Larry's body this morning." Lucy set her plate on the counter and hurried to the bunkroom, returning moments later with her cell phone in hand.

"I took pictures of the bunkroom, the crow's nest, the kitchen, the living area, the open deck and the marina dock." Lucy grew silent. "The slip next to us was empty when I snapped a picture last night. It was before you and Ruth headed to the office to pay for our spot."

"Which lines up perfectly with my theory that Larry or others knew the marina closed at nine. He, or his killer, slipped his houseboat in under the cover of darkness after the marina office closed."

"My gut tells me *if* Larry was still alive when he arrived at the marina, he wasn't alone," Ruth said.

After the women finished eating, they made quick work of cleaning up. Since the fish was cooked on the grill and the sides were prepared foods, there were only a few dinner plates and pieces of silverware to wash.

Liz hung back and watched the others clean the small galley kitchen. "Where are we spending tonight?"

"I was hoping to skip paying another slip fee," Ruth said. "We can head up river, closer to the marinas without pulling into one of the slips."

"Or we could pull a Larry, wait until the marina closes and sneak into an empty spot," Margaret said.

"Margaret," Gloria chided. "That's not right."

"I was joking. I don't care where we stay or if we have to pay."

"I would rather not stay at the Sunshine Bridge Marina." Rose frowned at Buddy's broken pole, propped up in the corner of the living room. "I need some time to think about how I'm gonna make it up to Buddy for breaking his favorite fishing pole."

"It's decided then," Ruth said. "We'll hang out close to the marina without parking in a slip." She headed upstairs to the flybridge while the others settled in on the sofas.

Restless, Gloria wandered out onto the open deck and gazed up at the clear skies. It wasn't nearly as warm, now that the sun was setting.

Oak trees, draped in moss and lining the riverbank, cast spooky shadows across the river.

Gloria turned as the slider opened. It was Liz. "Do you mind if I join you?"

"Of course not." She shifted to the side and Liz plopped down next to her sister. "Thank you for driving all the way over here to meet us."

"If I'd known you were roughing it, I probably would have passed. You know how I feel about outdoorsy stuff. My idea of roughing it is glamping."

"Glamping?"

"Glamour camping. Roughing it with all of the creature comforts like spa services, central air conditioning, room service..."

"Which is probably why Ruth didn't tell you," Gloria chuckled. "This isn't my idea of a dream vacation, but Ruth was excited and...I get to spend time with my friends, which makes this worth every minute of discomfort."

"I suppose. Ever since Frances went gaga over her new love, I find myself twiddling my thumbs these days."

"Are you homesick? Maybe you should think about moving back to Michigan."

165

Liz curled her lip. "I hate the cold."

"Then become a snowbird. Spend your summers in Michigan and winters in Florida."

"Martin might miss me."

"*Might?*" Gloria asked.

"He's been super busy lately. He hasn't been home much since he's been hitting the circuit and traveling all over the country for his golf tournaments." Liz picked at her fingernail. "I guess I am kind of homesick."

"And summer is right around the corner," Gloria pointed out. "Why don't you close up your house for the summer and head north?"

"I don't have the funds to buy another place and I can't afford to stay in a hotel for months at a time."

"I see." Gloria got an inkling her sister was hinting at staying with her. There was no way she could handle having Liz under the same roof for a couple of days, let alone the entire summer. She snapped her fingers. "Why don't you look into house sitting?"

"House sitting?"

Gloria warmed to the idea. "Hear me out. You could find some nice, swanky lakefront digs where the owners are traveling the world while you take care of their home."

"I...I hadn't thought about that." Liz shifted. "Do you think there are people in West Michigan who do that sort of thing?"

"Of course. I would start looking in a beach town like Grand Haven or Holland. Those people have some bucks."

"You might be onto something. Wouldn't it be fun?" Liz asked. "I could come back for the summer and we could hang out together."

Gloria gazed into her sister's eager face, the realization of what she'd proposed sinking in.

Liz moving back to Michigan...what was she thinking?

Ruth ran out to join them. "Liz. I was inside talking to the others and came up with a brilliant idea. I'll need your help."

"What kind of help?" Liz narrowed her eyes.

"I'll explain my plan to you first thing tomorrow morning, after I have a chance to iron out all of the details."

Chapter 12

Gloria slept with one eye open. She wasn't sure if it was the movement of the houseboat, the fear that at any moment a gator, snake or other river creature was going to slither on board...or maybe it was Liz's loud snores coming from the bunk directly across from hers.

She flipped over for the umpteenth time and pounded her pillow.

"Gloria, are you awake?" Lucy leaned her head over the top bunk and peered down at her best friend.

"Yes...unfortunately. I can't sleep."

"Me neither." Lucy's head disappeared. Her feet appeared and she slid off the bunk, landing with a dull *thunk* on the rug below. "Maybe a little fresh air will help."

"Let's go."

The sound of the window air conditioning unit muffled their exit from the bunkroom. Gloria led the way as they passed through the cozy kitchen and tiptoed through the living room where Dot was sound asleep on the sofa.

She eased the slider open and the women stepped onto the open deck.

Despite the humidity, there was a chill in the air.

Gloria rubbed the goosebumps on her arms before grabbing a beach towel and wrapping it around her shoulders.

She settled onto the bench seat. Lucy plopped down beside her and gazed up. "Look at all of those stars."

Gloria let out a small breath as the stars twinkled down, illuminating the night sky. "What a beautiful night for stargazing."

"It is."

Off in the distance, Gloria spotted the lights from the Sunshine Bridge Marina. "Tomorrow night is our last night on board the houseboat before heading to the beachfront resort."

"I must admit I'm looking forward to a little more luxury and pampering," Lucy said. "Although this was more fun than I thought it would be, except for dealing with Larry Molson's death."

"The authorities will clear Ruth soon," Gloria said confidently. "They have zero evidence. So what if Larry and Ruth exchanged a few words? It's not enough evidence to pin the murder on her."

"Did Dot tell you she saw Ruth out on the deck last night, all alone?" Lucy asked.

"She did. She was probably up for the same reason we are...she couldn't sleep."

"True." Lucy changed the subject. "I feel bad for Rose and the busted fishing pole. Rose feels terrible."

"She does, but if the fishing pole was Buddy's favorite, he shouldn't have let her borrow it." Gloria tucked the towel under her legs. "Liz is thinking about moving back to Michigan."

"You're kidding."

"Nope. She admitted she's lonely down here. Frances moved in with her boyfriend. Liz's boyfriend, Martin, and I hesitate to call him that because he doesn't sound like much of a boyfriend, is traveling all over the country on the golf pro circuit, leaving Liz alone."

"What about her place here in Florida? Can Liz afford to buy a second home up north?"

Liz, along with Gloria, Margaret and their long lost cousin, David, unearthed some valuable coins on their Aunt Ethel's property in the Smoky Mountains. After a lengthy legal battle with the State of Tennessee over the rightful ownership of the coins, David, an attorney, won the fight, making each of the women and him a million dollars richer.

"I have no idea what Liz did with her money, other than buy an expensive sports car and a dream home in a gated community." Gloria remembered the time a desperate Liz showed up on her doorstep, begging her sister to help her track down her wayward boyfriend after he vanished.

Before vanishing, Martin managed to weasel some extravagant and expensive gifts out of Liz. "She claims she doesn't have enough money to purchase a property in Michigan."

Lucy lifted a brow. "Did you offer to let Liz stay with you?"

"Are you crazy?" Gloria laughed. "I love my sister, but the two of us living under the same roof would be Fourth of July fireworks every day. I suggested maybe she could look into house sitting."

"I like the idea. Maybe she'll find some swanky digs over on Lake Michigan."

"My thoughts exactly. A beachfront bungalow would be right up Liz's alley." Gloria grew quiet as she thought about her sister's predicament.

Liz somehow managed to get under Gloria's skin in a way no one else could. Since she'd moved to Florida, their relationship had improved. "I think she's going to look into it."

Splash. Gloria bolted upright. "Did you hear that?"

"Yeah." Lucy wiggled off the cushion. She tiptoed to the railing and peered over the side of the boat. "I wonder if Eleanor's gator is nearby."

A small voice whispered from the shadows. "Did I hear someone say gator?"

"Eleanor?" Gloria peered into the darkness.

"Yeah." Eleanor emerged, sporting a pair of silky pajamas and reeking of an unpleasant odor.

Gloria plugged her nose. "What is that smell?"

"I'm trying to lure the alligators closer to the houseboat."

Lucy leaned in and took a whiff. "This is what's stinking up the bunkhouse closet. I thought someone dumped rotting fish inside. All along it was you."

"It's Rose's fish bait. I rubbed a little on my nightshirt, thinking if it worked with fish, it might work with gators."

Splash. The women heard another loud splash.

Lucy handed Eleanor a flashlight. "I heard something over there. The smell may have worked a little too well."

"I also tossed a handful of bait nuggets in the water." In her haste to get close to the water, Eleanor stumbled on a pair of flip-flops and almost tumbled over the side of the boat.

Gloria lunged forward and grabbed hold of Eleanor's arm, pulling her back. "Whoa there. If you're not careful, you're going to see your gator up close and personal right before he eats you."

"Sorry. I lost my footing in all of the excitement." A bit more cautious this time, Eleanor carefully leaned over the railing, her hands trembling as she held the night vision binoculars to her eyes. "Something is out there. I see eyes. I'm sure it's an alligator. Where's my cell phone? I want to take pictures."

Eleanor ran inside the houseboat and returned a short time later, followed by a bleary-eyed Margaret, Dot and Rose. "I woke them up in case they wanted to see the gators, too."

"What about Liz and Ruth?"

"Ruth didn't want to come down. When I tried to wake Liz, she punched me." Eleanor shook her head. "She gets cranky when you try to wake her up."

"Sounds about right," Gloria muttered. "You better get over there before your gators take off."

"I wonder how many are out there." Eleanor kneeled on the cushioned seat and began snapping pictures, the bright flash of the camera illuminating the murky waters.

Gloria caught a glimpse of sets of eyes. "Did you see that? There must be half a dozen gators out there!"

"You don't think they'll try to climb on the houseboat." Dot eyed the water nervously.

"I hope not."

"This is sure as heck makin' me nervous," Rose declared. "Those gators are most likely mean *and* hungry."

Eleanor began humming as she crept toward the front of the boat. "I see a couple more up here. One of them is the granddaddy of them all." The light from her phone lit up the large gator, who was circling the side of the houseboat.

177

"Eleanor, your scent is bringing them a little too close for comfort," Gloria said. "You should change your clothes."

"Not yet. I need a couple more pictures. I want to get a clear shot of the big one. I'm going to print it off and stick it on my bucket list bulletin board."

The other gators, as if being signaled by the larger one, swam closer to the houseboat.

"I think Ruth is going to have to move the houseboat to get away from the gators." Gloria clamped onto Eleanor's arm. "Please go change before the gators try to board the boat."

"I suppose." Eleanor appeared crestfallen.

"Now you can definitely check this off your bucket list."

Something bumped the side of the houseboat. A bolt of fear ran down Gloria's spine at the thought of a gator boarding the boat and attacking them.

"That does it." Rose disappeared inside. She returned in a flash, waving a tall, thin plastic container. "I'm sorry, Eleanor, but I'm not about to be eaten by a gator and neither are any of my friends."

Rose unscrewed the top of the container and dumped a handful of dried leaves in the palm of her hand. She flung the leaves over the side of the houseboat before hurrying to the other side.

One of the gators lunged forward, his snout bumping into the metal hook on the front of the boat.

Seemingly unfazed by the gator's aggression, Rose tossed another handful of her concoction into the water.

Finally, the gators began to retreat.

"That did the trick, Rose. I think they're leaving," Gloria said. "What's in there?"

"It's a mix of hops for making beer, deer urine, cottonseed and my secret ingredient - garlic. Won't hurt the gators, but most critters don't like the taste. At least it works on the deer who are always after my flowers."

"The big guy up front...he's not going anywhere." Lucy jabbed her finger toward the front of the houseboat where Eleanor stood transfixed as she and the massive gator stared each other down.

"I think he's trying to tell me something," Eleanor whispered.

"He's trying to tell you he's hungry." Rose eased past Eleanor and tossed two handfuls of her mixture off the front of the boat. The large gator flipped over and then sank below the surface.

"See you later, big guy," Eleanor said wistfully. "I think he liked me."

"He wanted to have you for a midnight snack." Concerned for her friend's safety...and possibly her sanity, Gloria led Eleanor away from the front of the boat and to the slider doors. She opened the door and nudged her inside. "Please take off those pajamas and put them in a sealed bag."

"And take a shower," Margaret said. "You smell awful." She waited for the door to close behind Eleanor. "We're going to have to keep an eye on her."

"Hopefully, her fixation with gators is over." Gloria sank onto the bench. "I'm sorry Eleanor woke you."

"No biggie. I was half awake." Margaret waved her hand. "It's hard to sleep through Liz's snoring."

"Maybe we should suggest she trade places with Dot and sleep on the living room sofa tomorrow night," Rose said. "I think I saw an air mattress in the hall closet. We can put it on top, so it won't hurt Liz's back."

"That's an excellent idea." Gloria reached over and patted Rose's hand. "Thanks for getting rid of the gators. I guess we won't be going for a midnight dip in the river."

After Eleanor finished showering, the women climbed back into their bunks. Gloria pulled the covers over her head to drown out the sound of Liz's snores.

Before she drifted off to sleep, she prayed God would give them a restful rest of the night, that they would enjoy their last day on board the houseboat and last, but not least, they would figure out who murdered Larry Molson.

Early the next morning, the women fixed a hearty breakfast of bacon, eggs, toast and pancakes. Although everyone insisted Rose and Dot sit back and let someone else do the cooking for a change, it didn't last long. Soon, both were in the kitchen helping prepare the food.

Since this was their last full day on board the boat, Ruth asked each of them for a suggestion on what they wanted to do.

Liz was bored by the laid-back list and decided to hang out inside and read. Rose's only request was to return the fishing pole to Buddy, the sooner the better.

Ruth was looking forward to cruising up and down the river. Eleanor claimed her next major bucket list items were driving on the beach in a convertible and sky diving.

Dot was also perfectly content to relax on the houseboat and read.

"What about you, Margaret?" Gloria asked. "What would you like to do?"

"I would like to visit Crimson Hall, but not to see a ghost. I love antiques and collectibles. I was able to do a little research on my phone. It looks like an interesting place."

"I'm with Margaret," Lucy said. "But I want to go for the history and the haunting. What about you, Gloria?"

"I want to visit Crimson Hall, too. I want to go there for a completely different reason. I also did a little more research on my phone this morning and found out something very interesting about Crimson Hall."

Chapter 13

"You discovered Crimson Hall isn't crimson," Lucy joked.

"No." Gloria shook her head. "Crimson Hall was once owned by Joyce Jameson."

"Who is Joyce Jameson?" Rose asked.

"Oh no. Here we go," Margaret mumbled.

Gloria shot Margaret a pointed stare. "Joyce Jameson is an amazing actress. She's the lead actress in the award-winning series, Detective on the Side."

"She's a sleuth," Rose surmised.

"Not just any sleuth. Joyce is a super sleuth. She inspired me to get started in solving mysteries. She doesn't own the estate now. I'm not sure if she ever even stayed at the place. From what I read, she had big plans to restore it to its former glory, but never made it out of Hollywood long enough to follow through. She sold it to the county and that's when they started the restoration process."

"Your only reason for wanting to visit this place is because of Joyce Jameson?" Ruth asked.

"Of course not," Gloria said. "I also want to track down the mysterious Indian, Soaring Eagle. He was one of the last people to see Larry Molson alive. I want to ask him a few questions."

Ruth's cell phone beeped and she glanced at the screen before picking it up. "Great. It's Detective Flanders." She hurried outside and slid the slider shut behind her.

The women watched as Ruth traipsed back and forth, gesturing wildly. A short time passed before she pulled the phone away from her ear and stepped back inside.

"Well?" Lucy asked.

"I told Detective Flanders everything we uncovered so far. He wants to meet with me again later today or tomorrow. He claims he has a few more questions to ask me after speaking with the owners of the Sunshine Bridge Marina as well as the man who was working the night Molson died."

"Buddy," Rose interrupted.

"Yes, your buddy, Buddy. The detective also talked to several people who were at the Gator House Landing the day Molson and I argued. Molson told several people I intentionally damaged his houseboat and that I threatened him."

"That's not true," Gloria said. "You have eyewitnesses who saw the whole thing - us. You didn't intentionally damage Molson's houseboat. I wouldn't call giving him the middle finger when he gave it to you first, a threat."

"When are you meeting the detective?" Dot asked.

"I told him I would have to get back with him." Ruth turned to Liz. "Are you still up for a little sleuthing?"

"You never elaborated on what you want me to do. Plus, you know I'm not good at investigative work," Liz whined. "Snooping into other people's business is more Gloria's thing."

"I scheduled an appointment with Ike Molson at the Molson & Molson Investigative Agency for ten o'clock this morning. I thought about having Gloria meet with him, but she doesn't have a Florida address or ID," Ruth patiently explained. "Molson thinks he's meeting Liz Applegate, a heartbroken, rich woman whose lowlife husband is cheating on her."

"But I'm not even married or have a wedding ring or anything," Liz argued.

"You can borrow mine." Rose promptly slipped her wedding band off her finger and handed it to Liz.

"Rose!" Lucy exclaimed.

"What? I'm not breakin' my vows. I'm loaning her my ring. Now don't lose it," Rose said.

"I won't. For the record, I'm one hundred percent against my involvement." Liz slipped the ring on. "If I screw it up, don't blame me."

"What matters is you're willing to try," Gloria said. "After the appointment, we can run by Crimson Hall to check it out. If we're lucky, Soaring Eagle will be there. Last, but not least, we'll stop by the Sunshine Bridge Marina and return Buddy's broken fishing pole."

"Don't remind me," Rose said glumly.

The women quickly washed their breakfast dishes, storing the leftover pancakes and bacon in the fridge. Ruth climbed the stairs to the flybridge to begin making their way back to the marina and the rental van.

When they reached the Gator House Landing, Ruth joined Liz and the others on the dock. "Wish us luck."

"We're going to need it." Liz started to follow Ruth and then abruptly stopped. She motioned to her sister. "You're going, too."

"Why? Ruth already explained you have to be the one to meet with Molson. All you have to do is pretend to be a heartbroken wife with a cheating husband."

"I still want you to go," Liz said stubbornly. "I know how your investigations fall apart. If I'm going down, you're going with me."

"Whatever. If it makes you feel better, I'll tag along and keep Ruth company."

"Not just tag along. You're going to the appointment with me - for moral support. Remember, I'm a heartbroken wife and I need my sister by my side."

"Fine. Have it your way. I'll go with you." Gloria ran back inside and grabbed her purse.

"We'll be here if you need us," Lucy called out.

"Thanks, Lucy." She followed Liz and Ruth to the rental van. During the ride to Orlando, Gloria attempted to give Liz pointers, all of which Liz completely blew off.

"If I'm going to do this, I need to do it in my own way, otherwise it won't be believable." Liz held out her hand to admire Rose's wedding band. "This is a pretty ring. I love the princess cut diamonds. I wonder where she got it."

"You can ask her later," Gloria said. "Now don't forget, the main reason you're there is to try to question Molson about his brother."

"How am I going to lead into a conversation about Larry Molson?"

"Fib," Ruth said. "Tell his brother you talked to Larry the other day. He promised to meet you to discuss the surveillance, you saw something on the news about a man who was found floating in the river and you're certain his name was Larry Molson."

"That should open up the conversation," Gloria added.

"But won't he become suspicious?" Liz wrinkled her nose.

"Not if you tell him you're concerned that your surveillance won't be handled properly. You could throw in some other stuff to try to get a feel for his relationship with his brother."

"Well, we all know how sibling rivalry can cause a rift."

"Then this will be right up your alley, sis."

When they reached the detective agency, Ruth circled the building before pulling into an empty spot near the back of the parking lot.

"Why don't you drop us off out front?" Liz asked. "I'm wearing heels and there are several potholes in the parking lot."

"Fine." Ruth rolled her eyes and backed out of the parking spot. She eased alongside the curb, stopping in front of the building's entrance. "I'll be right here and don't forget...you want to find out as much as possible about Larry Molson. You could even cry a little if you think it might help."

"I can't believe the things you and your friends get me into." Liz shot her sister a troubled look.

"You better get used to it," Gloria grinned. "If you move back to Michigan, you can look forward to more."

"Don't threaten me." Liz slid out of the passenger seat and slammed the door before tottering to the front entrance.

Despite the high heels, Liz moved at a fast clip and Gloria hurried to catch up.

"I knew I should've stayed home and met you for dinner or something."

"And miss all of this excitement?" Gloria held the door for her sister and motioned her inside.

*****

Liz cleared her throat and approached the receptionist's desk. "My name is Liz Applegate. I have an appointment with Mr. Molson at ten o'clock."

"I'll tell him you're here." The young woman lifted a finger and picked up the phone. "Mrs. Applegate is in the lobby for her ten o'clock appointment." She replaced the receiver and stood. "I'll show you to his office."

The woman led Liz and Gloria down a narrow corridor and stopped in front of the door at the end of the hall. She gave a quick knock and then swung the door open.

"Thank you." Liz grabbed her sister's hand and dragged her inside.

The room reeked of leather and men's cologne. Overstuffed leather chairs and floor-to-ceiling bookcases filled the office. In the corner was a mahogany bar area with a speckled quartz countertop.

Liz straightened her shoulders and breezed across the room, a slow smile flitting across her face.

"Mrs. Applegate." The tall, bearded man behind the desk joined her on the other side. "It's a pleasure to meet you." He took Liz's hand in a warm grasp, holding it a little longer than necessary. Liz's smile widened. "Mr. Molson. Thank you for fitting me in on such short notice."

She turned to Gloria, who was standing near the doorway. "I hope you don't mind. I brought my sister, Gloria, with me. I...I've been distraught lately and am having trouble driving."

"Of course. It's nice to meet you, Gloria." Molson shook her hand and motioned the women toward the chairs. "Please. Have a seat."

Gloria perched on the edge of the chair closest to the door while Molson made his way behind the desk.

There was an uncomfortable silence as he studied Liz. She began to squirm, certain that he had her pegged as a fraud.

Gloria broke the silence. "My sister has a...delicate matter she would like to discuss."

Liz laughed nervously. "I've never hired a private investigator before."

"You've come to the right place; although I've been sitting here asking myself what sane man would step out on a gorgeous woman like you."

Flattered, Liz pressed a hand to her chest and batted her eyes. "You are too kind, Mr. Molson. I...hope I'm wrong."

"Me, too - for your sake." Molson leaned forward and studied the single sheet of paper on his desk. "My notes say you suspect your husband of extracurricular activities and you would like my agency to investigate."

"Yes...Mart...Marty has been traveling extensively and spending a lot of time at the club...golfing. I want to make sure there's nothing funny going on."

"I see." Molson leaned back in his chair and crossed his arms. "Are those the only signs, extended travel and spending time golfing?"

"There's one more thing." Liz pressed her palms together. "I picked up his cell phone the other day and noticed several cell phone numbers I don't recognize. Local of course, but with no names. I was so flustered; I didn't think to jot the numbers down. Looking back, I should have."

Molson tapped the tip of his finger on his chin. "It sounds as if you may be in need of our services. Did my partner go over our rates?"

"As a matter of fact he didn't, which reminds me. I was supposed to meet Larry Molson. When I called to schedule an appointment, the receptionist told me he no longer worked here."

"My brother, Larry, was only working at the agency part-time." Molson paused as if searching for the right words. "He...retired."

"Retired?" Gloria perked up at Molson's explanation.

"He was semi-retired. Unfortunately, he passed away unexpectedly, which is the reason he's not meeting you today."

"I'm sorry to hear that." Gloria turned to Liz. "I told you I heard something on the local news about a man named Molson who was found dead in the St. Johns River the other day."

"I had no idea." A troubled look crossed Liz's face. "That's terrible. I'm so sorry for your loss. What happened?"

"I don't have all of the details yet," Molson said.

"But he was ready to retire?" Gloria prompted.

"Yes." Molson turned his attention to Liz's sister and their eyes met. "Gloria..."

An uneasy feeling settled in the pit of Gloria's stomach as Molson continued to stare.

"I've seen you somewhere before. You look very familiar."

Chapter 14

"Me?" Gloria began shaking her head. "I've never met you before. You must have me confused with someone else."

She quickly shifted the conversation back to Liz's predicament certain that at any moment Molson would realize he'd seen her at the Gator House Landing when Ruth ran into his brother's houseboat.

"All of this talk about infidelity is making me queasy." Liz abruptly stood. "I'll talk this over with my sister and get back with you in the next day or so."

Gloria joined her sister at the door. "Thank you for your time."

The women were silent until they reached the van. Liz scooched onto the passenger seat and slammed the door. "You almost blew our cover."

"I did not. I thought I handled shifting the conversation away from me quite nicely. You're partially to blame for insisting I tag along."

"What happened?" Ruth steered the van out of the parking lot and onto the street.

"We'll fill you in when we get back to the houseboat." Gloria dropped her purse on the floor. "Bottom line, we picked up a little information."

When they reached the marina, Lucy and the others were waiting for them on the deck of the boat. "Well? How did it go?"

"Liz did all right for her first assignment."

"What do you mean, I did all right?" Liz slipped Rose's wedding band off and handed it to her. "I was a rock star and now you owe me one."

"What did Molson say?"

"He wondered what a stunning woman like myself was doing in his office over claims her spouse was cheating on her."

"He was buttering you up," Gloria said. "He probably uses the same line on all of his female clients."

"That's a rude thing to say," Liz pouted. "Anyways, Ike told us his brother, Larry, was getting ready to retire and turn the business over to him. I'm not sure I believe him."

"Me, either," Gloria said. "Something isn't adding up."

"Molson's houseboat was parked right next to ours and yet none of us heard or saw a thing," Ruth pointed out. "I'm surprised someone didn't gun him down instead of taking the time to tie him up and dump him over the side of his houseboat."

"A gun makes too much noise, especially in such tight quarters, unless they used a silencer." Gloria rubbed the end of her nose. "Perhaps it wasn't premeditated."

"I did some research while I was waiting for you," Ruth said. "Molson & Molson Detective Agency is the two brothers, who both worked as detectives."

"We haven't looked into who Larry Molson may have been suing at the time of his death," Gloria said. "But first, we have more pressing matters. We still need to visit Crimson Hall and try to track down Soaring Eagle, one of the last people to see Molson alive."

"Daylight is burning." Ruth took her place behind the wheel of the houseboat and they began their journey toward Crimson Hall, which was farther along the river than Gloria thought.

Despite the big, billowing clouds giving off some relief from the scorching sun, Gloria could feel her nose starting to burn. She slathered a thick layer of sunscreen over her exposed skin and slipped her sunglasses on. "We've been riding for a long time now."

"You're right." Dot glanced at her watch. "I wonder if Ruth missed the landing." She slid off the bench and Gloria followed her inside. "Are we lost?"

"Sort of. I think I missed the turnoff," Ruth said. "We're also running low on gas."

"How low?" Gloria asked.

"Actually, we're running on fumes. I thought the tank was half full, but I misread the gauge."

"Didn't the Gator House Landing loan us gas cans for a backup?" Gloria started for the door.

"They're empty. I never bothered to fill them, figuring we wouldn't need it," Ruth said in a small voice. "I guess I miscalculated how much fuel we would use."

The houseboat slowed. The engine sputtered and then stopped.

Liz emerged from the bathroom, towel drying her hair. "What's going on? I smelled a strong odor coming in through the ceiling vent."

"They're the last fumes of gas we have in the houseboat," Gloria said.

"We're out of gas? How does that happen?"

"It happens when someone isn't paying attention and didn't fill up when we needed to," Ruth said.

"Now what?" Dot asked.

"There's an emergency riverside service number we can call. I saw their magnet on the fridge." Ruth stepped over to the refrigerator and ran her hand along the side. "Here it is. We'll ask them to bring us some gas, enough to make it back to the marina where we can fill up."

"I'll call." Dot pulled her cell phone from her pocket. "No, I won't. You're not going to believe this. I don't have cell service."

Ruth turned her phone on. "Me either."

*****

"You're kidding." Gloria pulled her phone from her purse and discovered she didn't have service either. She began to laugh hysterically at the thought of being stuck in the middle of the St. Johns River, out of gas with a boatload of women and no idea where they were, not to mention no way to call for help.

"It's not funny," Ruth frowned.

"Oh, it's funny." Gloria clutched her stomach. "I think this is perfect fodder for a scary story. Instead of calling this the houseboat, we'll nickname it the death boat. A group of women become stranded on a houseboat in the middle of the river. They're lost, out of gas and they have no cell service. Meanwhile, a serial killer is roaming the river, looking for unsuspecting victims and the women are sitting ducks."

"Your mind works in wicked ways." Dot shivered. "Thank goodness it's not dark yet. Now what do we do?"

"We wait until the houseboat drifts into an area with cell service or until someone comes along and helps us. I'll fill the others in on the good news."

Ruth stepped onto the open deck and briefly explained what had happened, apologizing several times.

"Don't you worry none, Ruth," Rose said. "We got plenty of food on board and eventually, someone will find us."

Despite their initial optimism, the river was deader than a doornail and not a single watercraft passed by during the first hour.

The women continued to check their cell phones as they slowly drifted along the river.

"Great." Ruth pointed to a band of ominous clouds that were beginning to gather. "A storm is brewing."

Low thunder began to rumble and when Gloria spotted a flash of lightning, the women headed inside. The wind picked up and nudged the houseboat toward the bank of the river.

"I think we should try to tie up and wait out the storm." Ruth opened the slider. A bolt of lightning flashed nearby and she jumped back. "Or maybe not."

"It's too dangerous to go out there," Gloria said nervously.

"I've never been on a river during a storm," Margaret said.

"Me either," Liz said.

Gloria had. Years ago, her first husband, James, had borrowed a friend's fishing boat and they'd gone out for a day on the river in nearby Green Springs. An unexpected storm popped up, almost sinking the small boat. It scared Gloria half to death.

The sudden storm was another reason she wasn't keen on fishing with Paul. Smaller boats offered little protection from violent storms. At least on the houseboat, there was some protection.

"Try to stay away from the windows," Lucy suggested.

"There are windows everywhere," Margaret said.

The skies let loose and buckets of rain poured down, along with flashes of lightning, one right after the other. Thunder shook the houseboat and Gloria began to pray. "Dear Lord, please protect us during the storm."

"Yes, thank you, God," Dot said.

"Amen," Lucy added.

"Maybe we should hang out in the bunkhouse where there aren't any windows," Ruth suggested.

"Good idea."

The women huddled in the bunkhouse as the winds and thunder continued to shake the houseboat.

Rain pummeled the roof and Gloria continued to pray.

Finally, she could hear the rain let up and the women ventured out into the living room. The skies were still dark with only light rain, accompanied by an occasional rumble of thunder. "I think the brunt of the storm has passed."

Gloria checked her cell phone again. "I still don't have a cell signal."

"On the bright side, the rental agent at the Gator House Landing will start looking for us tomorrow if we don't show up to return the houseboat," Ruth said.

The women discussed securing the houseboat and heading ashore to try to find help, but after stepping outside and surveying their surroundings, they unanimously decided they would be safer staying put.

"Who knows how far we are from civilization. Tromping through the thick brush and swampy surroundings could be dangerous," Dot said.

"Agreed," Ruth said. "We stay on board the houseboat. Someone will come along eventually."

Another hour passed, and the fast moving storm was long gone.

Liz, who was peering out the kitchen window, took a step back. "Let's play cards. I have a pack in my suitcase."

Thud. Thud. Thunk. A sudden rapping on the side of the boat interrupted their conversation.

"Someone is out there." Ruth ran outside and the others quickly followed behind.

Gloria, thrilled at the prospect of being rescued, began thanking God. Her excitement was short-lived when she reached the open deck and caught her first glimpse of their rescuer.

Chapter 15

The Army green Jon boat was as worn and battered as the man draped over its outboard engine. "You are stranded."

It was more a statement than a question and Ruth nodded her head. "We ran out of gas and can't call for help because we don't have cell service." She waved two large gas cans. "Can you give me a lift to the marina?"

"Ruth," Gloria elbowed her friend. "Are you sure you want to do that?" She hissed under her breath.

"Do we have a choice?"

The man in the boat, either not hearing the exchange or ignoring it, stood. His small boat caused a ripple in the water as he made his way to the front. "I can give you a lift to the marina."

Ruth didn't give him a chance to change his mind or her friends a chance to talk her out of it. "That would be great."

She handed him the gas cans and grabbed onto the railing of the houseboat before stepping into the smaller boat. "How far away is the marina?"

"Twenty minutes down river. It is the closest spot," he replied. "You will be back in less than an hour."

"Thank you..." Ruth's voice trailed off.

"Soaring Eagle. I am the caretaker at Crimson Hall."

"What a coincidence. We were on our way to Crimson Hall to take a tour." Ruth settled onto the bench seat and glanced back at her friends, who were hovering anxiously near the front of the houseboat.

A small niggle of fear crept into Gloria's mind. "Would you like me to ride with you?"

"We go alone," Soaring Eagle answered. "We can travel faster with less people." He flipped the motor on before swinging the boat around and heading down the river.

Liz watched as the small boat disappeared around the bend. "Did you see that rickety old contraption? Ruth will be lucky if they make it to the marina and back without sinking."

"I'm not sure I would've gotten into the boat with him." Margaret rubbed the sides of her arms. "Did you see the tattoo on the back of his neck? It looked like a snake."

"I saw it," Rose murmured. "My Great Aunt Lajaria had a great respect for the keepers of the earth, whom she also called friends. Ruth will be safe with Soaring Eagle."

"Is that where your great aunt got some of her potions?" Dot asked.

"Yes, from the Indians and also from the lowlanders, the bayou people," Rose said. "My aunt lived an interesting life."

Despite Rose's words of assurance, Gloria was concerned for her friend's safety and paced anxiously, waiting for Ruth's return.

Finally, she spied a small dot on the horizon. The dot grew bigger. It was the Jon boat, skimming lightly over the water and moving at a fast clip as it drew closer to them.

Ruth sat in the front of the boat, a big smile on her face. She gave her friends a small wave.

"See?" Rose said. "I told you Ruth would be safe."

Soaring Eagle cut the motor and they drifted toward the houseboat.

Gloria knelt down and grabbed hold of the front of the small boat. "You made good time."

"Soaring Eagle knows how to boogie." Ruth handed Gloria the gas cans and stepped onto the houseboat before turning back. "Thank you, Soaring Eagle, for taking me to get gas. We'll be along shortly for a tour of Crimson Hall and don't forget what I said about dinner tonight."

"You are welcome, Reckless Ruth. I will look forward to dinner prepared by you and your friends." Soaring Eagle turned the motor on and cruised out of sight.

Ruth carried the cans of gas to the back of the boat and began filling the tank.

Gloria joined her. "Will this give us enough gas to get back to the marina to fill it up?"

"Yep. It's on the way. We'll stop by Crimson Hall to tour the place before heading back to the Sunshine Bridge Marina to fill up. I figured we could return the broken fishing pole at the same time."

"It looks as if you and Soaring Eagle hit it off."

"Yeah." Ruth shook her head. "He's a character. He knows an awful lot about the river and the people in this area."

"Did you bring up the subject of Larry Molson?"

"Of course. Soaring Eagle didn't mince words about Molson. He said he was a troublemaker and mentioned that Molson was living on his houseboat."

"Seriously?"

"Yep. Soaring Eagle claims Molson's wife kicked him out of the house. He's been living on his houseboat for about a month."

"Did Soaring Eagle mention talking to Molson at the Gator House Landing the day of his death?"

"No. I didn't want to put him on the spot, and he didn't mention it." Ruth finished pouring the gas and then replaced the cap on the containers. "Like I said, Soaring Eagle knows a lot about what goes on around here, which was one of the reasons I invited him to dinner."

"That's an excellent idea, Ruth. We're running out of time. We need to step up our investigation if we're going to figure out who murdered Molson."

Ruth made sure everyone was on board the houseboat before settling in the captain's chair and steering the boat back toward the center of the river. They had only gone a short distance when Ruth turned into a shady cove.

A narrow boat landing was hidden beneath a canopy of majestic oak trees. There was a wooden placard on shore with the words, *Crimson Hall*, and an arrow pointing toward a steep set of cement steps.

"This is Crimson Hall?" Margaret made her way to the front of the boat.

"Yep. I never would've found it if Soaring Eagle hadn't pointed it out to me."

Lucy climbed onto the dock and grabbed the line to secure the houseboat. The women joined her...everyone that is, except for Liz.

"I think I'll hang out here and keep an eye on the boat."

"Are you sure?" Gloria asked.

"Haunted houses aren't my thing, plus those stairs are going to do me in." Liz pointed to her stiletto heels.

"You forgot to bring a more practical pair of shoes?" Dot asked.

"I have beach sandals, but I don't want to ruin them traipsing through the swampland to visit a moldy old manor."

"But..." Margaret started to argue and Gloria lifted a hand. "Let Liz stay. She won't enjoy the history of the place. We'll be sorry if we force her to come along."

"I think I'll take a nap while you're gone. Someone was snoring last night and it kept waking me up."

"It was you, Liz." Gloria said.

"Very funny. I don't snore." Liz lowered her sunglasses and sprawled out on the lounger as she slipped her wide brimmed hat down over her face.

"I'm not sure about this." Rose eyed the steps nervously.

"You'll be fine." Lucy, who was leading the way, stopped suddenly at the top of the steps. "Oh no."

"What?" Dot eased past her friend. At the top of the stairs and to the left was a small cemetery. "That must be the small cemetery Buddy mentioned."

Rose broke free from the group and took off running. She didn't stop until she reached a small footbridge several yards away.

The others hurried to catch up.

"I've never seen you run so fast," Dot teased.

"You ain't never seen me in front of a cemetery before." Rose set the pace, walking at a brisk clip as they crossed the bridge.

Beyond the footbridge was a narrow walkway. It meandered through a canopy of majestic oak trees. The tree line cleared, revealing a large, two-story Greek revival estate.

"I see several cars and a building over there," Ruth said.

"Hopefully, they have air conditioning." Margaret fanned her face. "I'm sweating to death."

The women stepped inside the building and the dark-haired woman behind the counter smiled. "Welcome to Crimson Hall. Are you here to tour the estate?"

"Yes." Gloria nodded. "We were hoping to cool off for a minute before starting the tour."

"Then I suggest you enjoy our short presentation on the history of Crimson Hall. Follow the signs down the hall and to the back. The presentation runs every ten minutes."

"Perfect. Thank you." Gloria followed her friends to the theater, a cool and welcome relief from the humid Florida heat.

Inside the theater, they watched a short video. It gave them a brief history of Crimson Hall, a 19th century hunting estate overlooking the St. Johns River.

The site was listed with the National Registry of Historic Places. Historians believed the caretaker's home was among the oldest intact buildings still standing in Central Florida.

A wealthy river merchant, who chose the river not only as his winter retreat, but also as a hunting lodge, built the hall in the late 1800's.

In its heyday, Crimson Hall hosted a number of the country's wealthiest citizens including Presidents Ulysses S. Grant and Grover Cleveland; the Astors, the Goulds, the Vanderbilts; and also the Prince of Wales, who went on to become King Edward VII.

The history of the estate was intriguing. Near the end of the presentation, the narrator explained the ten-acre estate included the eight-thousand square foot hunting lodge, horse stables, cabins for the estate employees and finally the caretaker's cottage.

After the video ended, the women returned to the gift shop to purchase tickets to tour Crimson Hall and the grounds.

Gloria reached into her wallet and handed the clerk a twenty-dollar bill. "I enjoyed watching the video on Crimson Hall's history. We heard the place is haunted."

"Yes. Rumor has it Crimson Hall is haunted by Edward T. Parker, the wealthy merchant who built the magnificent Greek revival and died inside the home."

"In a police shootout," Gloria prompted.

"That's the rumor. Whether it's true or not has never been verified. Other versions are Mr. Parker became despondent and depressed after the death of his wife, who died mysteriously, some say of yellow fever. He committed suicide a short time later." The clerk counted out Gloria's change and handed her an admission ticket. "I've seen him myself."

Eleanor squeezed in next to Gloria. "You have? What does he look like?"

"A ghost." The woman grinned. "He doesn't like crowds. I doubt you'll see him during your visit. Our caretaker, Soaring Eagle, has seen him numerous times, but only at night after the visitor's center closes and everyone has gone home for the day."

"We met Soaring Eagle when our houseboat ran out of gas," Ruth said. "If not for him, we would still be out on the river, waiting for help."

"Soaring Eagle spends most of his free time patrolling the river. There isn't much that goes on around here Soaring Eagle doesn't know."

Gloria thanked the woman and wandered out of the shop to wait for the others to join her.

Eleanor traipsed out of the building. "Did you hear that? If we have dinner with Soaring Eagle this evening, we might see an honest to goodness ghost."

"We're not coming back here tonight. Soaring Eagle is joining us on the houseboat," Gloria warned. "Plus, Mr. Parker doesn't like crowds."

The others drifted out of the store and joined them. They followed the path leading to the back of the house, where they climbed the porch steps. A guide wearing period clothing greeted them.

"Welcome to Crimson Hall." She led them inside, through the vestibule and into the spacious country kitchen. They paused while she explained how at the time the estate was constructed it boasted all of the state-of-the-art amenities.

The guide answered a few questions and then led them into the opulent dining room.

Margaret made her way to the center of the room and stood next to the dining room table. "This is a king cathedral walnut table in pristine condition."

"You have an eye for antiques. It's an exact replica with matching hand tooled leather chairs." The guide pointed to the ceiling. "The handcrafted crystal chandelier, made in France, isn't from the 1800s, but it fits perfectly above the table."

Gloria took a step back to admire the chandelier and the sparkling crystals. "It looks expensive."

"It is. All of the furnishings are irreplaceable. Both Crimson Hall and the grounds are heavily insured."

After she finished admiring the table, Margaret wandered over to the floor-to-ceiling bay windows. "These are beautiful windows."

"Almost large enough to walk through," Dot commented.

"These are indeed windows, which could be used as doors, as well." The guide explained that back in the 1800s, residents were taxed based on the number of doors in a home...the more doors, the higher the tax. "The more creative and wealthy landowners built their homes with exterior windows. They also functioned as doors to reduce the amount of property tax paid to the local government."

"Clever," Dot said.

The guide led them through the dining room to the parlor, followed by the soaring two-story front entrance before stopping in the library.

They wandered past a grand piano as the woman pointed out several portraits, along with the bell system used by the homeowners to summon the servants when needed.

The final room on the main floor was the sitting room. The upper level bedrooms circled a large center hall. In the back were separate servants' quarters.

After finishing the tour of the bedrooms, the guide started down the narrow back steps. She explained the servants used the stairs for easy access to the kitchen.

Dot tapped a long, narrow pane of glass. Behind the pane of glass was a square, wooden box. "What's this?"

"It's the dumbwaiter. The servants used it to move the guest's luggage from the back porch to the second level and the guest bedrooms. It's no longer operational."

The guide led them to the back porch, their original starting point and told them they were free to tour the grounds, the stables and the pavilion.

"What are those?" Gloria pointed to what appeared to be a row of storage buildings. At the very end was a cozy two-story cottage, painted pale blue.

"Those are storage buildings. The building at the end is the caretaker's cottage. It's a private residence and off-limits," the guide explained.

"Soaring Eagle's home," Ruth guessed.

"Yes, Soaring Eagle lives in the cottage. I don't believe he's here today. He spends most of his time on the river, making sure the boaters are behaving themselves and helping out those in need."

"Like a bunch of women who run out of gas," Rose muttered.

Gloria chuckled. "True."

"I have a question." Eleanor stepped forward.

"Yes?"

"The ghost, Mr. Parker. We heard he haunts Crimson Hall. Have you ever seen him?"

The guide shifted her feet. "As a matter of fact, I have met Mr. Parker, upstairs in the master bedroom. It was in the evening, after a Christmas party and I was locking up."

The woman hesitated. "Some people think I'm crazy."

"I don't think you're crazy," Eleanor said.

"Well, as I said, I was upstairs making sure all of the lights were off and I felt a cool breeze blow by me. I thought someone followed me upstairs, but there was no one there. I switched the lights off in Mr. Parker's private bathroom and when I turned around, he was standing there...except I could see right through him."

Dot clasped her hands. "That would've scared the daylights out of me."

"I wasn't scared. He was only there for a moment and then..." The guide snapped her fingers. "Poof. He was gone."

"That's a good ghost story," Margaret said skeptically.

"Believe what you will." The guide smiled. "Some believe, some don't. It's not my job to convince you. I'm here to share the history of Crimson Hall."

"And you did a wonderful job." Lucy handed the woman a generous tip. "Thank you for the awesome tour. So far, this has been my favorite part of our trip."

The guide joined a new tour group and the women wandered the grounds before making their way back to the houseboat.

Liz was in the same spot, her sunglasses in place and wide-brimmed hat still covering her face.

She woke with a start as the women began boarding the houseboat. "How was it?" Liz covered her mouth to hide a yawn.

"It was very interesting," Gloria said.

"Did you meet Parker's ghost?"

"No, we'll do that later, when we come back here to meet Soaring Eagle," Eleanor said.

"Are we coming back here later?" Rose asked. "It will be dark."

"And creepy," Dot chimed in.

"I promised Soaring Eagle a homemade dinner, or as close as we can get," Ruth said. "If not for him, we would still be sitting on the river, waiting for someone to come by and help us."

231

"I think it's a great idea. We can kill two birds with one stone," Gloria said. "We can pay Soaring Eagle back for rescuing us and find out what he knows about Larry Molson."

There was a small chiming noise and Gloria reached for her cell phone.

"It's mine, Gloria." Rose snatched her phone off the counter. "Well, butter my biscuits."

"Who is it?" Dot peered over Rose's shoulder. "I hope it's not Johnnie or Ray, calling with an emergency."

"It's Buddy from the marina. He's probably calling to find out when I'm returning his fishing pole. What should I tell him?"

Chapter 16

Before her friends could answer, Rose ended the call. "I gotta think about what I'm going to say to him."

She picked up the broken fishing pole and ran her hand over the thin layer of duct tape. "I feel terrible. Can someone deliver the damaged pole to Buddy with my sincere apologies?"

Gloria draped a loose arm around her friend's shoulders. "It will be fine, Rose. Accidents happen. We'll apologize and offer to pay Buddy for the broken pole. We'll be sure to tell him how awesome the pole and his bait worked before the pole broke, trying to reel in the big one. I say we do it the sooner, the better. You've been letting this bother you all day."

"It's still bothering me. Maybe he left a message, telling me to keep the pole." She tapped the front of her cell phone and held it to her ear. "He didn't leave a message."

Ruth settled into the captain's chair. "Might as well put Rose out of her misery and head to the marina."

Rose grabbed the pole and made her way onto the open dock. She dropped onto the bench seat, her shoulders hunched.

"Poor Rose." Gloria stared at her through the slider. "I'm sure Buddy will understand it was an accident."

It was a short ride to the Sunshine Bridge Marina. Ruth was getting the hang of handling the boat. Slick as a whistle, she slid in between two speedboats docked near the center.

Rose reluctantly made her way to the front of the boat and Lucy joined her. "I'll go with you, Rose. Don't forget Buddy's tackle box."

"I better make sure nothing is missing." Rose set the busted pole on the dock and opened the tackle box, rummaging around inside. "There wasn't much in here except for a small roll of duct tape and a box of crappie lures."

Liz plopped down on the bench seat to watch. "I wouldn't tell him you think his lures are crappy."

"No...not crappy, crappie. C-r-a-p-p-i-e - lures for crappie," Rose patiently explained. "It's a kind of fish."

"Crappy...crappie." Liz waved her hand. "I'm definitely not an expert on fishing."

"Here you go. The duct tape got mixed in with the tote the Gator House Landing loaned us." Ruth handed Rose the tape. "Good luck."

"Thanks." Rose picked up the fishing pole while Lucy carried the tackle box. The women trudged to the end of the dock.

Dot sucked in a breath. "This fishing pole thing has been weighing heavy on Rose's mind. She'll feel much better after she talks to Buddy."

"I hope he doesn't give her too hard of a time about the pole," Margaret said. "It was an accident."

"I hope not, either." Gloria meandered along the dock, stretching her legs when she caught a glimpse of Lucy and Rose, racing back to the boat at a quick clip. "What happened? Was Buddy ticked off and he chased you out of the office?"

"No. We never got a chance to talk to Buddy. The police hauled him off to jail. The marina owners, the Buchanans, are in the office. We overheard them talking. They claimed they were missing money from the cash register. After questioning Buddy and doing a background check, the authorities discovered he had an outstanding warrant and arrested him."

Gloria sank down on the bench. "Maybe he did murder Molson."

"Maybe, maybe not," Ruth said. "Remember, Larry Molson didn't have a reservation for a slip. Dot told us his name wasn't written in the book."

"Which makes it an even greater case against Buddy," Gloria said. "Think about it. Buddy could claim he had no idea Molson was even in the marina."

"But why kill him here?" Lucy asked. "He would be a prime suspect."

"I don't think Buddy killed Molson," Rose said. "I guess he tried to call me right before the authorities showed up."

"I don't believe Buddy is the culprit, either. We don't know what the warrant was for, so it's mere speculation." Dot shook her head. "He's too obvious of a suspect."

"Along with his brother," Gloria said. "Ike Molson said his brother was retiring and planned to live on his houseboat."

"Which brings up another point...where was Molson's estranged wife during all of this?" Liz asked. "Perhaps she's a suspect."

"The list of suspects is growing. I think I need to start writing them down." Gloria grabbed a pen and a piece of paper. "Ike Molson, Larry's brother, is a suspect. The fact he and his brother argued puts him at the top of the list, not to mention the fact they were business partners. Maybe Ike wanted him out of the way."

"Don't forget his wife since she seems to be MIA," Lucy said. "Soaring Eagle, too. He was with Molson shortly before his death."

"And the owner of the other marina, Mr. Paver. Darcy, the server, claimed the man who owned the Gator House Restaurant and Gator House Landing didn't care for Larry, either," Ruth pointed out.

Gloria jotted the names on the sheet of paper before looking up. "Personally, if I had that many issues with a patron, I would ban them."

"Like the time I almost banned Judith Arnett from the restaurant?" Dot chuckled. "Sometimes it's best to let sleeping dogs lie. If he continued to cause problems, well then I would rethink the situation."

"Poor Buddy." Rose slumped down on the bench. "He seemed like such a nice man."

"So that means we don't have to meet up with Soaring Eagle and try to glean information from him?" Liz asked.

"No. I promised him dinner and I plan to keep my end of the bargain," Ruth declared. "Which reminds me, what's for dinner?"

The women scrounged through the refrigerator, trying to figure out what to have. They'd only bought enough food to last until the morning, when they would return the houseboat and embark on the second half of their vacation.

"I remember seeing a meat counter in the marina store," Dot said. "They looked like pretty good cuts of meat."

"Steaks sound good. We can use the rest of the charcoal while we're at it," Ruth said.

"Perfect," Dot said. "I'll go get my purse."

"We can share the cost." Ruth followed her friend inside.

"Ruth, you've done more than your share. You bought the gas. You paid for the slip space the other night. Dinner is my treat."

"Are you sure?"

"I insist."

Gloria joined them. "I want to help pay, too." She grabbed her purse and she and Dot made their way along the dock to the marina store.

Fitz, the owner, was behind the counter, talking to a woman. The conversation ended when Dot and Gloria stepped inside.

The woman abruptly turned on her heel and stormed out of the office, slamming the door behind her.

Dot and Gloria exchanged a quick glance before heading to the meat cooler in the back. While Dot perused the selection, Gloria headed to a bin of potatoes.

She counted out the potatoes and then swung by the freezer section to grab some garlic bread.

She joined Dot, who was filling a shopping basket with thick cuts of sirloin steak. "Do you think these potatoes will work?"

"Yes, they're perfect. All we have left to buy is a carton of sour cream for the baked potatoes and a dessert."

"I saw some cream pies, right next to the garlic bread." Gloria returned to the freezer section, reached inside and pulled out two chocolate cream pies. She balanced the loaves of garlic bread on top of the boxes of pie and carried them to the cash register where Dot stood waiting.

"I think that will do." Dot nodded approvingly. She turned to Fitz, the owner. "I think we have everything."

"Let me help pay," Gloria fumbled in her purse and pulled out some cash. "Those steaks are expensive."

"Expensive and well worth it," Fitz said as he reached for the groceries.

Gloria handed Dot two twenty-dollar bills. "I'm sorry to hear your employee, Buddy, was arrested."

Fitz paused, his hand midair. "You know Buddy?"

"My friend, Rose, borrowed Buddy's fishing pole the other night and we stopped back by here to return it. That's when we heard the police arrested him. I'm sure he had nothing to do with Molson's murder," Gloria blurted out.

"How did you hear about Mr. Molson?"

Gloria tightened her grip on her purse. "We were staying here at the marina the night of Larry Molson's death."

"Have you talked with the authorities? They're questioning everyone who was here. Say..." Fitz's eyes narrowed. "I thought I recognized you...you were on the houseboat with Ruth, the woman who found Molson's body."

"Yes, that was me."

"My wife called the police to report money missing from the till. When they got here, they started asking Buddy a bunch of questions and ran a warrant check on him." Fitz shook his head. "He swears it's a misunderstanding. The authorities decided to take him to the precinct for questioning. Buddy shouldn't have been arrested."

"He seems like a nice man." Gloria remembered the tense exchange between Fitz and the woman when they entered the store. "I'm guessing from your wife's reaction a few minutes ago she doesn't agree."

"You could say that." She could tell Fitz Buchanan was becoming agitated. "I'm sure the authorities will clear Buddy after they've had a chance to straighten this mess out. I knew I should've kicked Molson out the last time he raised a ruckus around here." Fitz counted out Dot's change and handed her the receipt.

"We'll be praying for Buddy." Gloria grabbed their grocery bags and exited the store. She waited for Dot to join her and closed the door behind them. "He was ticked."

"Fitz and his wife were arguing," Dot said.

"Yep, and ten bucks says it was over Buddy."

The women unloaded the groceries while Ruth eased the houseboat out of the marina. "It shouldn't take long to get back to Crimson Hall."

"Hopefully, just enough time for a quick, late afternoon siesta." Gloria shoved the empty grocery bags in a drawer and slipped onto the open deck.

The gentle roll of the river was relaxing. She curled up on the seat and closed her eyes before drifting off to sleep.

The houseboat lurched and Gloria jerked her head up.

The slider flew open and Lucy emerged. "Houston, we have a problem."

"What kind of problem?"

"We have to go back to the marina."

Chapter 17

Gloria blinked rapidly, trying to clear her head. "Why do we have to go back to the marina?"

"Because Ruth forgot to get gas and we're coasting on fumes."

"Again?"

There was a nervous silence on board the houseboat as Ruth drove them back to the marina.

As soon as the marina was in sight, Gloria let out the breath she was holding.

"I'll tie up the boat." Lucy headed outdoors.

Ruth descended the spiral staircase. "I'm sorry. I forgot all about getting gas after Rose started telling us about Buddy's arrest. I was in such a hurry to meet Soaring Eagle on time, it completely slipped my mind."

"It's okay, Ruth," Eleanor said. "I forget stuff all of the time. I want to pay for the gas. It's my turn."

"Are you sure?" Ruth asked.

"Absolutely." Eleanor grabbed her backpack and followed Ruth to the gas pumps.

Despite having to backtrack, they managed to make it to Crimson Hall at six o'clock on the dot.

Ruth emerged from the crow's nest, cell phone in hand. "I texted Detective Flanders to let him know we were on the river. I told him I could meet him tomorrow morning at the Gator House Landing when we drop off the houseboat."

"Perfect," Gloria nodded approvingly. "That buys us some time to talk to Soaring Eagle."

"Can we check out the caretaker's cottage?" Eleanor asked. "I was hoping we could pay another visit to Crimson Hall after it closed."

"It was Soaring Eagle's idea to meet us at the houseboat. I don't think he wanted us inside his house," Ruth said.

"Maybe he's messy," Lucy guessed.

Liz leaned her hip on the counter and gazed out the slider doors. "I think I see someone coming down the stairs now."

Ruth ran out to greet him while Dot began preparing the steaks.

Gloria scrubbed the potatoes, placed them on a plate and then into the microwave before turning it on.

While the potatoes cooked, she turned the oven on and pulled the loaves of garlic bread from the fridge.

"The loaves of bread are bigger than the oven," Margaret said.

Gloria opened the oven door and peered inside. "It is tiny. I guess I'll have to cut the bread into more manageable pieces." She sawed the loaves in half and then arranged them on a baking sheet.

While Gloria worked on the hot foods, Lucy pulled the chocolate pies from the freezer and set them out to thaw.

Liz sat at the counter and watched the others work.

"You could offer to help," Gloria said.

"You're doing quite well without me getting in the way."

"Fine, we'll put you in charge of clean up after we eat."

"I'm company," Liz insisted. "An invited guest."

"Who invited you?" her sister asked.

"Ruth. I'm Ruth's guest."

"Guests still need to pitch in and help."

Liz curled her lip and then her expression softened. "Martin sent me a text. He misses me. I think I'm going to skip the oceanfront condo and head home."

"Darn," Gloria said sarcastically. "We're going to miss you."

"That's the most insincere remark you've ever made."

"Ladies." Lucy stepped between the sisters and held up her hands. "We're sorry, Liz, that you won't be joining us at the resort. Gloria said you're thinking about house sitting in Michigan this summer, so we'll see you soon."

"Yes. I'm going to find a place to house sit," Liz said. "When I get settled in…"

"If," Gloria interrupted.

"Oh no. I will," Liz said confidently. "With my stellar credentials and a recommendation from Judge Brian Sellers."

"Retired Judge Sellers. Besides, Brian is my friend, not yours. You barely know him."

Liz gave her sister a sinister look. "Are you done interrupting?"

"Yep," Gloria smirked. "Carry on."

"*When* I get settled in, I'm going to invite all of you over."

"It sounds like fun," Margaret said. "Try to find a place with lake access if you can. Any number of spots would be perfect for a summer retreat."

Ruth escorted Soaring Eagle inside. She introduced him to the women while Gloria filled glasses with iced tea and soda.

Ruth and Soaring Eagle chatted while Gloria and Dot cooked the steaks on the portable grill they'd set up outdoors.

Finally, the food was ready. The women bowed their heads and Ruth prayed. "Dear Heavenly Father. Thank you for this food. Thank you for letting Soaring Eagle find us earlier today. We also thank you for this time of fellowship together, time to share with friends. We pray for Larry Molson and his family, and that his killer be brought to justice. Most of all, we thank you for our Savior, Jesus Christ."

"Amen," A chorus of amens went up and then the women began eating as Soaring Eagle regaled them with stories of misadventures on the St. Johns River. "There is always someone needing help on the river."

"Including a boatload of women," Gloria joked.

Soaring Eagle smiled. "You are some of the more appreciative ones." He cut off a large piece of steak. "Thank you for the dinner. It's delicious."

"You're welcome," Ruth said.

"Is Crimson Hall haunted?" Eleanor asked.

Soaring Eagle studied Eleanor's eager face. "Maybe."

"Do you know how Mr. Parker died?" Gloria remembered the story of the owner being involved in a shootout with the authorities and a second version where he committed suicide because he was heartbroken after his wife's death.

"I don't know. It is one of the great mysteries of Crimson Hall." Soaring Eagle's cell phone beeped. A look of concern crossed his face. "Excuse me. I need to step away to take this call."

He set his plate on a side table and hurried off the boat. He stood a distance away, a somber expression on his face.

"Uh-oh. It looks like he got some bad news," Ruth said.

Soaring Eagle returned a few moments later. "I'm sorry. I must eat and run. Something important has come up." He inhaled the last few bites of steak.

"I hope everything is all right," Lucy said.

Soaring Eagle glanced at the darkening skies. "I must take care of an urgent matter before it gets too late. You must leave the landing. Visitors are not allowed after dark. Thank you again for the meal."

He jogged off the houseboat, raced up the steps and disappeared from sight.

"That was odd," Margaret remarked.

"It sounded urgent," Rose said.

"I agree. Did you notice how he made a point of insisting that we leave?" Gloria ate the last few bites of her food. She wandered into the kitchen and set her dirty plate in the sink before returning to the deck area where the others were finishing up.

"I'll help with clean up," Margaret offered.

"Liz will, too." Gloria gave her sister a pointed stare.

"I had my nails done yesterday."

Gloria lifted a brow.

"And it cost a small fortune."

"Then you can dry." She waited for Liz to finish eating and then followed her inside to make sure she didn't try to weasel her way out of kitchen duty.

Gloria nearly collided with Ruth, who was on her way back out. "Is everything all right?"

"Yes. I'm waiting for Lucy to untie the boat, so we can get going."

"Are we heading back to the Gator House Landing, so we'll be there early to drop off the houseboat?" Dot asked.

"No." Ruth shook her head. "Not yet. We're stopping somewhere else first."

Chapter 18

"Where are we going?" Gloria peered out the window and into the murky darkness.

"I don't know yet," Ruth said.

"We're driving around aimlessly?"

"Of course not." Ruth consulted her cell phone.

Lucy, who had been sitting on the open deck with the others, joined them inside. "It looks like we're heading back to the Sunshine Bridge Marina."

"Maybe," Ruth said.

"We're not going to the marina?" Lucy shook her head, confused.

"We're following Soaring Eagle. I noticed his boat parked not far from ours. I planted a small tracking device on it, thinking he might leave Crimson Hall and my hunch was right. I don't want him to see us. Turn off the exterior deck lights."

"I hope you know what you're doing." Lucy grabbed a flashlight off the counter. She darted to the back of the boat and flipped the lights off.

The slider opened and Margaret stuck her head inside. "Why did you turn the lights off?"

"Ruth is in hot pursuit," Liz said.

"At least give us a flashlight before Eleanor falls off the side of the boat, looking for more gators." Margaret held out her hand.

Gloria grabbed a second flashlight off the counter and handed it to her.

"What's going on?" Rose nudged Margaret out of the way and stepped into the living room. "It's darker than the dickens out there."

"We're hot on the trail of a suspect," Gloria said.

"I noticed right after Soaring Eagle took the phone call, it seemed like he couldn't get rid of us

257

fast enough," Ruth said. "I figured something was up, so while everyone else was cleaning up, I decided to attach a tracking device to the back of his boat and follow him."

"Where did you get a tracking device?" Gloria shook her head. "Never mind. You brought some spy supplies with you."

"Of course," Ruth said. "I never go anywhere unprepared. Soaring Eagle seemed to skip all over the subject of Larry Molson's death. He never mentioned he was with Molson the day of his death and now this."

Ruth picked up her cell phone and stared at the screen. "He's turning into the Sunshine Bridge Marina."

"If we're trying to avoid detection, why don't we pull off near the gas pumps and snack shack," Lucy suggested.

"Sounds like a plan. We'll tie up near the end of the dock area and then we can proceed on foot."

When they got close, Lucy grabbed the ropes and handily secured the boat, using the marina's lights to see.

"What if he's armed?" Dot glanced over her shoulder. "If Soaring Eagle is involved in Larry Molson's murder, who's to say he won't kill again?"

"We'll need some sort of weapon," Gloria said.

Eleanor handed her a marshmallow fork.

"What will this do?"

"You can poke an eye out."

Lucy reached into the toolbox and pulled out a hammer. "This might work."

"You better be able to swing quick if the perp gets close to you." Ruth strode to the back of the boat and returned carrying a can of pepper spray.

"You spray them and I'll conk them over the head with the hammer," Lucy said.

"While I poke their eye out," Eleanor said.

259

"How in the world did you get a can of pepper spray on the plane?" Gloria asked.

"Pepper spray isn't allowed in carry-on bags," Eleanor said. "I checked."

"I didn't bring it on the plane. I bought it at the gift shop in the airport when you guys were in the bathroom," Ruth said.

"They sell pepper spray in the airport?" Margaret wrinkled her nose.

"Only in Florida," Liz mumbled.

"We need to get a move on." Ruth, pepper spray in hand, made her way to the slider. She eased it open and crouched low as she crept onto the dock.

"We can't all go," Gloria said. "Lucy and Eleanor have weapons, so you stick close to Ruth. I'll follow a few steps behind in case I have to call 911."

"If you don't return in the next half an hour, I'll call the police." Dot waved her cell phone.

"Give us forty-five," Ruth said. "Unless you hear us screaming."

"Or gunshots," Lucy said. "Definitely call if you hear gunshots."

"You are all crazy." Liz flung herself on the bench seat. "The police already have Molson's murder wrapped up and a suspect in custody. I think you're chasing your tails *and* harassing an innocent man."

"Thanks for the unsolicited opinion," Gloria said.

"Fine. Whatever," Liz shrugged.

"I need my backpack." Eleanor hurried back inside and returned, backpack in tow. "I'm ready to go."

Gloria waited until Lucy, Eleanor and Ruth were several steps ahead before darting to the edge of the dock and following behind. As she walked, she scanned both sides of the marina, keeping her ears open for the sound of footsteps or voices.

A couple of times, she lost sight of her friends as they stayed close to the buildings, slowly making their way to the front.

When she neared the front of the marina, Gloria caught a glimpse of Soaring Eagle's small Jon boat.

Up ahead and near the entrance to the marina store, she spotted a bright flash of light. Ruth must've seen it too. She ducked behind a clump of bushes.

Gloria's breath caught in her throat as she waited for her friends to keep moving.

The light flashed again.

Gloria picked up the pace as Ruth and the others disappeared around the back of the office. She followed them to the end of the building and peeked around the corner.

The women had vanished.

"How can I keep an eye on them if I can't keep up with them?" Frustrated, Gloria jogged to the other end of the building. "Ruth?"

Quick footsteps clattered on the cement walkway and then abruptly stopped.

Gloria squeezed her eyes shut as she said a small prayer, certain they were about to be busted. The only sound she could hear was her heart pounding loudly in her chest.

The seconds crept by before the person turned back and the footsteps faded. Gloria let out the breath she was holding when she spotted Ruth's silhouette near a thick hedge.

She sprinted to her friend's side. "What are you doing?"

"Trying to figure out what's upstairs. We followed Soaring Eagle here. He was looking in the windows of the marina store and then he went up the stairs."

"There's something upstairs," Lucy added.

"Did he try to break in?" Gloria asked.

"No. He tiptoed up the steps and then peered in the windows," Ruth said.

"He tried the doorknob, too," Eleanor said. "Then he came back down, looked around and left."

Gloria motioned to the upper level. "I wonder what's up there."

"I don't know, but I'm going to find out." Lucy crept to the steps and hustled to the top.

Ruth started to follow. Gloria's hand shot out and she held her back. "No. Let Lucy do it. The fewer of us out in the open and exposed, the better."

"True."

Gloria watched as Lucy slipped back down the stairs and joined them. "It looks like an efficiency apartment. I could see a sofa and a small kitchenette."

"Did you happen to see which way Soaring Eagle went?" Ruth asked.

"No. I never saw him at all," Gloria replied. "The only ones I saw were you."

"He's probably getting away." Ruth strode around the side of the building. Lucy and Eleanor ran after her.

Gloria was only a few steps behind them when someone grabbed her arm and jerked her back. She felt the tip of a gun pressed against her skin.

"Are you looking for me?"

Chapter 19

Gloria's knees started to buckle as Soaring Eagle pressed the butt of the gun against the back of her neck. "I...no." She knew talking her way out of the situation was futile. She did the only thing she could think of, and that was to beg for her life. "I'm unarmed. Please don't shoot me."

Ruth, Lucy and Eleanor, hearing the commotion, turned back.

"Don't come any closer," Soaring Eagle warned. "I'm calling the cops."

"So they'll find our bodies after you shoot us?" Lucy wheezed.

"Why are you following me?"

The gun shifted slightly and for a brief moment, Gloria thought she might live to see another day.

"You were acting suspicious," Eleanor said. "Ruth placed a tracking device on your boat and we followed you here."

"I am after Larry Molson's killer." Soaring Eagle lowered the gun and released his grip on Gloria. Her knees gave way and she started to go down.

Soaring Eagle grabbed hold of her arm and propped her up. "You are weak."

"Because I just had the butt of a gun breathing down my neck," Gloria said.

"Buddy Granger is in jail, suspected of murdering Molson."

Gloria took a cautious step away from Soaring Eagle and his weapon.

"Something strange is going on around here. Buddy and I are good friends. He didn't kill Molson. He told me Larry Molson was hanging around the marina, acting like he owned the place. The Buchanans didn't charge Molson to stay here. I'm trying to figure out why."

267

"How are you going to do that?" Gloria pressed a light hand to her throat; thankful that Soaring Eagle didn't shoot first and ask questions later.

"Buddy hid a key to the office after he found out the authorities wanted to talk to him. He told me where to find the key and asked me to sneak inside the office to look for the reservation book."

"Is that what you were doing upstairs?" Ruth asked.

"Yes. He hid the key under the doormat. The upstairs unit is a vacant apartment, owned by Fitz and Caroline Buchanan."

"Well?" Eleanor tapped her foot impatiently. "What are we waiting for? Let's go back to the office and have a look around."

"I work better alone," Soaring Eagle said.

"We work better as a team," Ruth said.

Soaring Eagle noted the stubborn look on Ruth's face. "Four of us will draw more attention."

"I can be the lookout," Ruth said.

"I think I can handle this one." Eleanor shrugged off her backpack, unzipped the center section and pulled out a set of binoculars. "I brought my night vision binoculars. I'll be able to spot someone coming from a mile away."

"Way to go, Eleanor," Ruth grinned.

"These binoculars have night vision?"

Eleanor handed the binoculars to Soaring Eagle. He pressed them to his eyes. "They work."

"Of course they work," Eleanor snapped. "This isn't our first rodeo."

He handed them back. "Buddy is out on bail. His arrest warrant was old. The police have nothing to keep him, but they are trying to pin Molson's murder on him. The investigators claim they found a hidden stash of cash on Molson's boat. They believe Buddy found out about it and tried to rob him. Molson fought back and Buddy knocked him out, bound his hands behind his back and tossed him over the side of his boat."

Soaring Eagle told them Larry Molson bragged to Buddy he was working on a hot deal that would set him up for the rest of his life. "I think I know what it was that Molson was working on. Someone was paying him money."

"How do you know all of this?" Gloria remembered the comment Darcy, the waitress, had made that Soaring Eagle knew everything that happened on the river.

Soaring Eagle held up a hand. "I must hurry, before it's too late."

"Why are you in such a hurry? The office is closed until morning." Gloria's sleuthing radar went up. "I know why. You think someone is going to show up, Molson's killer, and you thought it was us."

"You must leave," Soaring Eagle repeated.

"No way." Ruth crossed her arms. "We...I have as much at stake as you do. Plus, we can back you up."

"I mean no offense, but you will get in the way."

"Because we're a bunch of senior citizens, and women at that, who have no clue what to do?" Lucy smirked.

"I am trying to catch a killer, something you have no knowledge of how to do."

Ruth burst out laughing. "And you have no idea who you're talking to."

Gloria patted Soaring Eagle's arm. "Let's just say we've solved a case or two on our own."

"Or a dozen or more," Ruth murmured.

"Gloria and her posse are the cream of the crop in mystery solving," Eleanor said.

"You're kidding," Soaring Eagle eyed them skeptically.

"I know what you're thinking. Times a wasting," Gloria said. "The marina is full of boats. Anyone could wander up here and catch us snooping around."

"Which is why we should be your lookouts," Ruth pointed out.

"I..." Soaring Eagle started to tell them he didn't need their help, but quickly realized they were going to give him a hand, whether he wanted them to or not. "Don't get in my way."

Eleanor, Ruth and Lucy split up while Gloria followed Soaring Eagle to the office's rear entrance.

"Is there an alarm?" Gloria whispered.

"Yes. It is two steps in and to the left. I have the code."

She followed him inside, ducking low as they tiptoed to the alarm. The steady *beep...beep* of the alarm grew louder.

Gloria squeezed her eyes shut, bracing herself for the inevitable blaring.

Soaring Eagle punched in a four-digit code and the beeping stopped.

He moved soundlessly through the back of the building before reaching a paneled door. The door let out a loud squeak and Gloria cringed.

They paused for a moment before Soaring Eagle motioned her into the office and he began sifting through the items on the counter.

"Did you find it?" Gloria whispered.

"Not yet. We will move faster if you check the other side."

"Right." Gloria sprang into action and began rummaging through a stack of papers. It was dark and hard to see.

"I think I found it." Soaring Eagle waved a binder in the air.

Two sets of bright headlights illuminated the front of the building and part of the office. It was followed by the sound of tires crunching on the gravel.

Chapter 20

Things moved fast after that. Soaring Eagle tucked the book under his arm. He lunged forward, grabbed Gloria's hand and dragged her out the back door.

Gloria had barely enough time to yank the door shut behind them before Soaring Eagle propelled her toward a clump of bushes where Eleanor was hiding.

"Hold this." Soaring Eagle thrust the binder in her hand before disappearing from sight.

"I was trying to warn you. I saw a truck and a car coming. They were speeding like bats out of you-know-what," Eleanor said.

"We made it out in time." Gloria struggled to catch her breath. "Now we sit here and wait until the coast is clear before heading back to the houseboat."

The minutes ticked by and Eleanor wiggled uncomfortably.

"Are you all right?"

"I'm fine." Eleanor reached into her back pocket. "But this is stabbing me in the rear." She pulled out a mini curling iron and set it on the ground.

"Why are you carrying a curling iron around?" Gloria shook her head. "Never mind."

"I stuck it in my back pocket earlier. I didn't want to clutter up the small bathroom counter and then I forgot to take it out."

"I figured it was the marshmallow skewer."

"Nah. I accidentally dropped that when Soaring Eagle stuck the gun against your neck." Eleanor began cracking her knuckles. "I've knocked two things off my bucket list now."

"The gator for sure." Gloria smiled. "What else?"

"Riding in an airplane. The last time I visited Florida, years ago with Matthew, we drove. The kids went with us and the trip took forever." Eleanor chuckled. "I think we stopped off at every rest stop from Michigan to Florida."

"That's a long drive," Gloria agreed.

"Riding with a carload of young kids makes it seem a whole lot longer." Eleanor was quiet for a moment. "Is Liz coming back to Michigan?"

"I think so. Frances is busy with her boyfriend and Liz seems lonely."

"I know how she feels. I get lonely, too. Not as much anymore now that I have you and the other girls to hang around. Your friendship has been one of the biggest blessings in my life."

Sudden tears burned Gloria's eyes. "Thank you, Eleanor."

"I guess we're still waiting for something to happen." Eleanor peered around the side of the bush. "I thought my life was over. Matthew was gone. The kids and grandkids, they have their own lives. My greatest fear was the thought of having to move out of my home and into a nursing home where I didn't know anyone. It's like the last stop...you know?"

"I...I had no idea you felt this way." Gloria's voice began to crack. "I'm sorry I didn't notice sooner."

"You were busy with your life. Everyone is busy with living life. It seemed to me as I got older, I started to slow down while everyone kept moving at a faster pace, and I was on the sidelines watching." Eleanor's voice was barely a whisper. "Looking back, I was depressed."

"What changed for you, Eleanor?" Gloria asked softly. "What was the turning point?"

"You and the other girls. At first, I admit I was envious when I heard the talk around town about how you and the other Garden Girls were solving mysteries and chasing down the bad guys. More than once, I almost picked up the phone to invite you over for coffee, but I knew you were busy."

"I don't ever want to be too busy," Gloria said. "I hope I never gave you that impression."

"You didn't. Maybe it was my pride telling me that. Then one day, you showed up on my doorstep with a bag full of fruits and vegetables. I'll never forget the day you sat at my kitchen table. We talked for a long time. Most people are in a hurry to get in and get out, but not you. You told me about one of the mysteries you solved."

"I did? I don't remember."

"Maybe not, but I remember. After that day, I said to myself, 'Eleanor Whittaker, no one can change your life but you. If you want to sit in this house and feel sorry for yourself, you have no one but yourself to blame.'" Eleanor patted her knee. "It wasn't even a month later that I noticed the unusual activity down at the Clemson cottage, right before they found Ed Mueller's body in the ice shanty."

"You were a huge help during that investigation," Gloria said.

"And it was my turning point, that and Rose's special elixirs."

The echo of voices quieted the women. Gloria parted the bushes, squinting her eyes to see. "Someone is out there."

They eased onto their hands and knees and began inching their way toward the back of the building. Gloria spotted two people standing near the bottom of the stairs. They climbed the steps and made their way inside the apartment right before the lights went on.

Gloria gingerly pulled her cell phone from her rear pocket and switched it on.

"Don't forget to make sure the flash is turned off," Eleanor said in a low voice.

"I hope they step near the window." Gloria held her breath, waiting for one of them to reappear. When they did, the man turned, giving her a clear view of his face. "Will you look at that?"

*****

The woman came up behind the man, slipping her arms around him.

Gloria zoomed in and snapped several more pictures before the man abruptly pulled the shades, blocking their view. "Did you see who that was? We're finally onto something."

From their hiding spot, Gloria had a partial view of the marina and Soaring Eagle's fishing boat as well as the back of the marina office. Eleanor and she stayed put until she spied Soaring Eagle stealthily making his way across the parking lot toward his boat.

Lucy, Ruth, Eleanor and Gloria joined him.

"Roy Paver, the owner of the Gator House Landing and the restaurant, and Mrs. Buchanan, the co-owner of the Sunshine Bridge Marina, are having a fling." Gloria briefly explained what Eleanor and she had seen. "I have several pictures and one where Mrs. Buchanan has her arms around Paver."

"It is beginning to make sense now. Buddy swears he could hear someone walking around upstairs, above the store at night, even though the apartment was vacant. Every time he went around back to check, the curtains were drawn and the apartment appeared empty."

Soaring Eagle pointed to the binder Gloria was holding. "Fitz Buchanan told the authorities he had no record of Larry Molson staying at the marina the night of his death. Buddy swears Molson told him he had a reservation."

"Why the cover up?" Gloria began to pace.

"Someone wanted it to look like Buddy let Molson stay and then murdered him. Mrs. Buchanan lied. She either somehow found out or knew about Buddy's previous criminal record and set him up."

"So Caroline Buchanan made it look like Buddy not only stole money from his employer, but also tried to rob Molson and then murdered him," Lucy said. "What does this have to do with Roy Paver, the owner of the other marina?"

"Larry Molson must have known about Caroline Buchanan and Roy Paver, and was taking money to keep quiet."

"Ah," Gloria whispered. "Darcy, the server at the Gator House Restaurant, told us her boss couldn't stand Larry Molson. I wondered why he didn't ban him from his establishment. Roy Paver couldn't because Larry threatened to expose the affair."

"Which explains why the investigators found a stash of cash on Larry's boat," Eleanor said.

"And why Buchanan claimed to have money missing from the cash register. Fitz Buchanan didn't know what his wife was up to," Lucy added. "But where do we fit in?"

Gloria snapped her fingers. "Because the original plan was to set us up for Molson's death. Don't you see? Larry Molson argued with us in the restaurant, right before Ruth rammed into his houseboat. I'll bet a hundred bucks that Roy Paver, the owner of Gator House Restaurant and the landing *and* Caroline Buchanan's lover, watched it happen."

She continued. "When Paver found out about our reservation to spend the night in the Sunshine Bridge Marina, he and Caroline Buchanan had the perfect opportunity to take Larry Molson out."

"But what are the chances Molson would end up docking right next to us?" Ruth asked.

"It wasn't by chance."

"Somewhere along the way, Paver and Caroline Buchanan changed plans. Buddy is picked up for a minor offense and was the perfect scapegoat," Lucy pointed out. "I'm sure the prosecutors think they have a slam dunk, an open and shut case and that Buddy murdered Larry Molson."

"It could be that Buddy was starting to question his bosses, why he was hearing noises upstairs in a supposedly vacant apartment," Gloria said. "Thinking that Buddy was onto them, Paver and

Caroline switched strategies and set Buddy up instead."

"What better person to blame than the employee who was working at the marina the night Molson died?"

"If the pictures I took turn out, we have some circumstantial evidence." Gloria waved her phone in the air. "It's no smoking gun, but it's a good start. Let's head back to the houseboat."

When they reached the houseboat, Dot met them at the door. "Well?"

"We think we're onto something." Gloria carried her phone inside and switched it on.

One of the pictures was blurry, but the rest were clear as a bell. The second picture was of Roy Paver and Caroline Buchanan climbing the stairs, another showed the apartment lights going on. The final picture was Roy Paver with Caroline Buchanan by his side.

Eleanor leaned over Gloria's shoulder. "Oh my. Your phone takes excellent pictures. What kind is it?"

"Thanks. It's an iPhone." Gloria turned it over. "They take great pictures."

"Let us check the reservation book." Soaring Eagle opened the binder. He flipped through the pages until he reached the previous Monday's reservation schedule, the one with Ruth's name on it. There was no reservation for Larry Molson.

"We have nothing," Gloria shook her head, her hopes dashed.

"Wait." Lucy grabbed the corner of the binder. "You haven't checked everywhere." She shoved her hand behind the binder's cover sheet. "I...think I feel something."

Gloria's heart skipped a beat as Lucy pulled out a folded sheet of paper. "What is it?"

Her excitement was short-lived.

"It's blank." Lucy held it up. "Sneaking into the office and borrowing the binder was a bust."

"We have nothing." Gloria started to close the cover.

"Not true," Eleanor insisted. "We have a clear shot of Caroline Buchanan and Roy Paver romantically involved. If Buddy can convince the authorities that he was hearing noises upstairs at night, perhaps the investigators will decide to question Paver and Caroline Buchanan.

Soaring Eagle held up a hand. "Fitz Buchanan doesn't appear to be involved. I would think he could corroborate at least some of Buddy's claims."

Gloria lifted a brow. "And he can verify whether or not his wife was home at the time of Molson's death. It's time to call Detective Flanders."

"I'm going to meet him in the morning," Ruth reminded them.

"Don't you think the authorities catching Caroline Buchanan and Roy Paver in the act would be better?" Gloria asked.

"True." Ruth whipped her phone out of her pocket and dialed the detective's cell phone number. "Now if only he'll answer."

The detective didn't answer, but as soon as Ruth disconnected the call, Detective Flanders called back.

With a quick explanation of what had transpired, she was able to convince the detective they were onto something, and that he needed to come by the marina as soon as possible to confront Roy Paver and Caroline Buchanan. She told him where the houseboat was parked and assured him they would stay put until he got there.

Gloria waited until Ruth disconnected the call. "Thank goodness he took you seriously. The sooner we get the evidence to the authorities, the sooner we can get back to our vacation."

*****

Gloria peered through the front window of the van and stared at the Sunshine Bridge Marina office. "What is taking them so long?"

"Here they come now," Ruth said.

The women waited until Rose climbed into the passenger side of the van while Dot climbed in back.

"What did Buddy say about his fishing pole?" Ruth asked.

"He wasn't mad."

"He gave Rose a big hug," Dot teased.

"If not for Soaring Eagle and the rest of us, poor Buddy would be in prison for the rest of his life, convicted of a crime he didn't commit," Gloria said. "I still can't believe Roy Paver and Caroline Buchanan tried to set us up."

"And when that didn't work out, they set poor Buddy up," Lucy said.

"They may have gotten away with murder if they hadn't made one fatal mistake."

"Trying to pin it on us," Lucy joked.

"Paying Molson in cash. When the authorities caught the two of them together after finding the stash of cash on Molson's houseboat, and then uncovered missing money from both marinas, they had enough evidence to bring Caroline Buchanan and Roy Paver in for questioning."

"And they might've gotten away with it if the lovebirds hadn't tried to pin the blame on each other," Ruth said. "Poor Fitz Buchanan. He was working a second job to make ends meet, and his wife was running around on him."

"He's better off without her," Margaret said.

"It's time to get the houseboat back to the marina and start the second leg of our Florida adventure," Ruth said.

"And we better not find any more dead bodies," Dot said.

Chapter 21

"Well?" Eleanor draped her arm over the side of the hot pink mustang convertible, her face beaming. "How do I look?"

"You look fabulous," Gloria said. "I want to get a close-up of your face."

"But then you won't see the ocean or the hot car."

"Fine. I'll take a close-up and one farther away and let you decide which one you want to frame." Gloria snapped a few more pictures. "I wonder how Liz is doing. I felt kinda bad about dropping her off at her place."

"But she wanted to go home to wait for Martin," Ruth reminded her.

"Hopefully, he'll show up." Gloria had been looking forward to meeting her sister's on-again, off-again boyfriend, but he'd backed out of their coffee date at the last minute.

"She'll be fine." Eleanor opened the driver's side door. "Everybody...get in."

"We all can't fit in the car," Lucy argued.

"Sure we can." Margaret grabbed her hand. "There's plenty of room." She climbed in the back seat.

Lucy followed her in. Next, it was Ruth, Dot, Rose and finally Gloria, who squeezed onto Dot's lap in the front seat.

Eleanor hopped behind the wheel and they cruised along the sandy beach, the smile never leaving her face. "This...this is the best day ever. I can't believe I'm cruising Daytona Beach in a pink convertible with my best friends. The sun is shining and I feel alive."

Eleanor's voice carried along with the waves and her happiness was contagious.

It *was* one of the best days ever. What more could anyone want than to be surrounded by good friends and enjoying the best years of their lives...the sunset years?

"Yes, Eleanor." Gloria closed her eyes and breathed in the ocean air. "This is one of the best days ever."

"After this, we're going parasailing." Eleanor flipped the visor down and caught Lucy's eye. "You're still going parasailing with me, right?"

"Yes, Eleanor. We're still going parasailing," Lucy said.

"While you do that, I'm going to grab my beach bag, a good book, an iced tea and settle in for some real relaxation." Gloria rubbed her hands together.

"Which reminds me," Ruth said. "When I dropped the houseboat keys off, the rental agent gave me a twenty-five percent discount coupon off my next rental. There's another marina down in the Keys the guy's brother manages. What do you think about renting another houseboat again next spring, but in the Florida Keys?"

"Oh no." A collective groan went up.

Gloria reached behind her and squeezed Ruth's arm. "I think we'll let someone else take a crack at planning our next girl's trip."

Eleanor stomped on the brakes. Gloria flew forward, whacking her forehead on the dash. "Eleanor."

"Sorry. A seagull darted out in front of the car."

"It's okay." Gloria tugged on her seatbelt. "Back to the next girl's trip. It won't be for a while. We have to start working on Andrea's baby shower."

"I miss her," Lucy said.

"Me, too," Dot agreed.

"We'll have to make sure to invite her on our next adventure," Gloria said. "She can bring the baby."

"On one of our adventures?" Rose's eyes grew wide. "Brian won't let that happen. No sane parent is gonna let their child run the roads with us."

Gloria shifted in her seat. "Of course Brian will. The baby is going to have seven doting grandmothers and the adventures of a lifetime. Mark my words."

The end.

If you enjoyed reading "Framed in Florida," please take a moment to leave a review. It would be greatly appreciated. Thank you.

The series continues...Book 22 in the "Garden Girls Cozy Mysteries" series coming soon!

Books In This Series

Garden Girls Cozy Mystery Series

Get Free eBooks and More

Sign up for my Free Cozy Mysteries Newsletter to get free and discounted books, giveaways & soon-to-be-released books!

HopeCallaghan.com/newsletter

Meet the Author

Hope loves to connect with her readers! Connect with her today!

Never miss another book deal! Text the word Books to 33222

Visit **hopecallaghan.com/newsletter** for special offers, free books,
and soon-to-be-released books!

**Pinterest:
https://www.pinterest.com/cozymysteriesauthor/**

**Facebook:
https://www.facebook.com/authorhopecallaghan/**

Hope Callaghan is an author who loves to write Christian books, especially Christian Mystery and Cozy Mystery books. She has written more than 50 mystery books (and counting) in five series.

In March 2017, Hope won a Mom's Choice Award for her book, "Key to Savannah," Book 1 in the Made in Savannah Cozy Mystery Series.

Born and raised in a small town in West Michigan, she now lives in Florida with her husband.

She is the proud mother of one daughter and a stepdaughter and stepson. When she's not doing the thing she loves best - writing books - she enjoys cooking, traveling and reading books.

Grilled Fish Recipe

<u>Ingredients</u>:

4 pieces raw fish, thawed (we used swordfish)

4 cloves garlic, chopped

¼ cup lemon juice

2 tablespoons soy sauce

2 tablespoons olive oil

1/3 cup Worcestershire sauce

1 tsp. liquid smoke

Salt and pepper to taste

<u>Directions</u>:

-In a glass baking dish, combine all of the ingredients, except for the fish

-Place fish in marinade.

-Refrigerate for at least one hour, turning frequently. (We marinated for five hours.)

-Preheat outdoor grill on high.

-Coat the grate with a light amount of oil. (We use disposable grill mats – highly recommend them) ☺

-Grill fish for 5 to 6 minutes on each side or until done.